KT-512-728

THE
FIRE
THIEF
FIGHTS BACK

SPARTAM · NACTUS · ES HANC · EXORNA

LORETTO SCHOOL LIBRARY

For Nicky Potter, with thanks.

KINGFISHER
An imprint of Kingfisher Publications Plc
New Penderel House, 283–288 High Holborn
London WC1V 7HZ
www.kingfisherpub.com

First published by Kingfisher 2007
2 4 6 8 10 9 7 5 3 1

Text copyright © Terry Deary 2007
Illustration copyright © David Wyatt 2007

The moral right of the author has been asserted.

All rights reserved. No part of this publication may be
reproduced, stored in a retrieval system or transmitted by
any means electronic, mechanical, photocopying or otherwise,
without the prior permission of the publisher.

A CIP catalogue record for this book
is available from the British Library.

ISBN: 978 0 7534 1470 5

Printed in India
1TR/0207/THOM/MAR/50CM/C

THE
FIRE
THIEF
FIGHTS BACK

TE ARY

Loretto School
13388

KINGFISHER

ONE

The first part of my tale is from a book of legends. "Hah!" you say. "Legends are just old lies. I want to know the TRUTH." Well, I have met one of the legends and I know that HIS story is true. So why shouldn't the other legends be true? Anyway, it's the only way we can explain what happened to me when I was a boy. And THAT was true, because I was there at the time. SO let's start with Ancient Greece and stop interrupting me with your moaning about the "truth" will you?

"What do you want, fat face?" the young god asked. He wore a winged helmet and had wings on his heels. He carried a rod with a snake wrapped around it. Even the snake looked shocked.

"You can't sss-speak to your mother like that, Hermes!"

"Oh, go shed your skin, you rat-tail of a reptile," Hermes replied and polished his nails on his white tunic.

"You'll be sss-sorry you sss-said that," the snake hissed. A goddess lay on a golden couch and scowled at the winged god. She was so beautiful you could hardly bear to look at her. Her dark hair fell in a curling cloud over her shoulders yet she never used curlers and hardly ever had to dye it.[1]

If you *could* bear to look at her, you'd have seen her face turn red with rage and her lips pull back tightly over her gleaming teeth. (And she never had to go to a dentist.) Somehow she controlled her temper.

"I am Hera, queen of the gods, wife to the mighty Zeus and ruler of the world. Speak to me like that and I will punish you like no god has ever been punished, Hermes."

He blew on his nails and gave a warm smile. "Oh,

---

1 Her hair was pretty good for a woman who was thousands of years old. In fact she didn't start dyeing it till she was 5,000 years old. But then she was quite a wicked goddess. Which just goes to show it is true what they say. Only the good dye young.

knock it off, Mum. You won't punish your dear little Hermes."

"Why not?" she spat.

"Because you *need* me! I am the messenger of the gods. If you didn't have *me* to run errands you'd be tramping from here to the Caucasus, from Troy to Atlantis, just to make mischief."

She narrowed her eyes. "Mischief?"

"Yes. You *know* you like to go around making trouble because you get *bored*, don't you, Mum?"

She raised her beautiful chin and looked through the window of the marble palace to the lake below and the mountains beyond. "Mischief is my job. It's what gods do."

Hermes walked across the shining marble floor, his winged sandals fluttering. He leaned over the goddess. "Anyway, you must *want* something or you wouldn't have *called* for me."

"Maybe."

"Oh, come on. What is it? You want me to kidnap some human maiden who's caught Zeus's eye? It wouldn't be the first time."

Hera glared at him, then her face went softer and almost tearful. Her voice was low. "It's more serious than that, Hermes. Zeus has gone."

The winged god threw back his head and laughed. "Gone? So? He's always off somewhere, the old goat. He'll be back. He always comes back to Olympus."

Hera blinked away a tear. "Not this time, Hermes. Not this time."

She looked around to make sure there were no servants watching and reached under the couch. She pulled out a scroll of yellow parchment and unrolled it carefully. Hermes peered at it. There was a message there but not in the usual ink and stylus.

"What's this?" Hermes asked. Even the snake stretched its neck to look.

Hera explained. "Someone has taken a different scroll, cut out the letters and stuck them onto the parchment."

"They'll ruin the scroll!" Hermes sighed.

Hera shook her head. "What has that to do with anything, idiot boy? The point is they sent this message."

"But why didn't they just write it?" Hermes asked.

"Because they didn't want us to know who sent it!" Hera said wisely.

Hermes nodded and read the message:

Dear Hera,

I have captured Zeus. I cut out the tendons in his wrists and knees. He cannot run. He cannot throw his thunderbolts. He is helpless. He is a prisoner in Delphyne's cave. I will not tell you where he is unless you bring me his crown so I can rule the world. You have until sunset to obey or Zeus will lose an eye, an arm or a leg every day till on the last day he loses his head. I mean it. The crown, or your hubby gets it... and I don't mean a holiday in Crete.

Yours sincerely,

The secret kidnapper – The Typhon

Hermes turned pale as his feathers. "The Typhon? The most hideous creature in all the world! And now he's going to rule the world."

"Not if you set Zeus free," Hera said softly.

"Not if I set Zeus free," Hermes agreed. Then he swallowed hard. "*ME!*" he squawked. "This is a job for a *hero* – Heracles or Prometheus. Someone who doesn't mind being blasted by a hundred dragon breaths. I'm a messenger, Mum! Why should *I* go? Why can't someone *else* rescue Zeus?"

Hera grabbed her son by the front of his tunic.

"Keep your voice down. Listen. Everybody hates Zeus…"

"Well, I wouldn't say *everybody*, Mum. I know *you* do…"

"If Hades in the Underworld gets to hear about this he'll be up here like one of your father's thunderbolts. He's always wanted to rule the Earth. And Poseidon down in the sea would leap like a dolphin at the chance. We've already had to defeat the revolting Giants…"

"Ugly brutes," Hermes agreed. "Their mother, Gaia, was furious!"

Hera nodded her head quickly. "And that's why Gaia created the Typhon – for revenge." She shook the letter under Hermes' nose. "This is it."

"But you still aren't saying why *I* have to go after the Typhon, Mum. He's a monster."

"He's half man," Hera shrugged.

"Oh, yes!" Hermes squawked. "It's not the man-half I'm worried about! It's the half that has a hundred fire-breathing dragon heads under his arms and the serpents that are wrapped around his legs!"

"Nothing wrong with sss-serpents," Hermes' snake hissed.

10

"There is when they can stretch out as high as his head – and he's as tall as this palace!" Hermes moaned.

"Sss-sorry, I'm sss-sure!"

"Every one of those dragon heads spits fire," Hera explained. "He can heat rocks with his breath and throw them at you."

The snake sighed. "I can't do that."

Hera turned to Hermes. "You are the only one I can trust. If Poseidon or Hades takes over Olympus they'll destroy you."

"*Me?* What have *I* ever done? I'm only a poor little messenger of the gods. I never did anyone any harm. Not one single god," Hermes whimpered.

"You are the son of Zeus and that is enough," Hera explained. "They will crush you – or shut you down in Hades' Underworld forever."

Hermes shuddered. "But how can a little old feathered fool like me beat a serpent-snapping, fire-frizzling fiend like the Typhon?"

Hera lay back and thought. "First you have to find your father…"

"But the Typhon says in the letter he won't say where Zeus is hidden."

"The letter also says Zeus is a prisoner in

Delphyne's cave. The Typhon isn't very bright."

Hermes looked miserable. "Are there no heroes brave enough to fight the Typhon? Someone who could battle with the monster while I sneak into the cave?"

Hera shook her head. "When the Typhon first appeared the gods all fled into Egypt or disguised themselves as animals."

"Chickens," Hermes mumbled.

"Yes, chickens – or rabbits or ducks," Hera agreed. "Only Prometheus would have been brave enough to tackle the Typhon."

"Even Prometheus is hiding," Hermes sighed.

"Ah, but he's not hiding from the Typhon," Hera said. "He stole fire from the gods and gave it to the humans. He is being hunted by the eagle-winged Avenger."

"Can't we bring him back? Offer to pardon him if he rescues Zeus?"

Hera shook her head. "He's travelled through time – he's thousands of years in the future. If the Avenger can't find him then we have no chance. Only Zeus could track down Prometheus… and Zeus is a prisoner of the Typhon. It's your job. You're Zeus's son."

Hermes puffed out his cheeks and blew. "And a son's got to do what a son's got to do. I'll go and get my maps," he said and fluttered sadly out of the great marble room.

The god Prometheus was also flying. Flying far out in the galaxy of stars. A strange monster flew by his side. A man with fifty heads on top of his square body and a hundred arms – fifty down each side. He was the guardian of the gates of the Underworld – the Hecatonchires – and he was escaping.

The two legends slowed as they reached an amber sun and headed for a planet of blue grasslands and green seas.

"Here we are, Hec," Prometheus said as they swooped down towards a village on the planet. "Your home planet."

Head number 35 sniffed away a tear. "Home," he said. "The prettiest word ever invented."

"Except the word 'prettiest'," head 27 argued.

Head 35 ignored him. "A planet where everyone has fifty heads and a hundred arms."

They hovered in the clouds. "I'm sure you'll be very happy here," Prometheus said.

"Oh, I will," head 35 said. "You could join me, Theus. The Avenger would never find you here."

"I'd feel a bit out of place," the hero demi-god sighed. "I'd be treated like a monster."

"Well, I suppose you are – only one head and two arms. You *are* a bit freaky."

"Thanks," Prometheus muttered.

Big Hec nodded fifty heads. "But I know what you mean. I was like that on Earth. People treated me like some weird alien! Me! I reckon *they* are the weird ones!"

"I can't imagine why."

"Because I have a hundred arms!" the Hecatonchires cried. "I mean, even your spiders have eight arms and as for your millipedes…"

"Yes, Hec. I'm glad you've found a planet full of your own sort," Theus said and looked down sadly.

"You'll find a home somewhere, Theus," head 49 said. "But I have a feeling it will be back on Earth. All you have to do is find a human hero and Zeus will set you free."

"I know," Theus said and nodded his single head. "I've been to that place they call Eden City. I've visited it twice now. I'm sure the answer lies down there. I went there in 1858 and again in 1795. Maybe if I go back just a little further… just ten years."

"That's 1785!" the Hecatonchires told him.[2]

"Then 1785 it is," Theus said and slapped the 100-armed monster on the back. "Goodbye, my friend. I hope you find happiness… but forgive me if I don't shake hands with you." He laughed. "It would take too long!"

As the Hecatonchires let himself drift down to the green and blue planet he waved a hundred hands in farewell.

Theus soared back to the edge of the universe and turned left at the farthest star. That way he would arrive back on Earth ten years before he left it in 1795.

He sped past meteors and comets through the emptiness towards a little planet that wasn't green and blue like the Hecatonchires' home. It was blue and green. "Home," he cried. "A pretty word."

But as he raced down towards the sunset side of Earth the god found there is a lovelier word than "home".

It's the word "hope".

2   The Hecatonchires was good at counting because he had a hundred hands and five times as many fingers. He could count up to… er… a lot. Then he could go on to use his toes and count up to a-lot-plus-ten.

TWO

EDEN CITY – 1785

You don't believe in legends? Then what about history books? There it is. 1785 the year of Freedom. We'd fought a vicious war against the king who ruled us from over the ocean. He was a madman who'd never been to or seen our country. We'd beaten him! We called it The War for Freedom. Of course after we drove out his soldiers and his cruel rule, we were left to make our own laws. There will always be crafty criminals who will travel around looking to lie and cheat and rob. People like me and my ma.

Eden City didn't have much to do with the War for Freedom. Nobody fought over it because there was nothing worth fighting for.

It was a jumble of tumbled houses and taverns,

shops and shipyards on a river. The streets were ankle-deep in mud in the winter and ankle-deep in dust in the summer. When Ma and I arrived it was autumn so it wasn't too bad. We stepped off the ferry from the river and wrinkled our noses at the sour smell of rottenness.

"Let's look around for a good place to set up, Sam," she said. We left our handcart with an old sailor on the waterfront and set off.

The only stone building in the city of warped wood was the jailhouse. "Make sure we don't end up in there," Ma said as we walked past it.

It didn't look half so bad as the houses. It seemed as if someone had built a house then decided it was too small. So they built another house on top of the first one. Then another... then another. Like houses of cards – and they looked just as likely to fall in a breeze.

But a house of cards gets narrower the higher you go. Eden City houses just got wider. They almost touched at the top so the roads and alleys below were gloomy and damp as a water rat's burrow. The sun never shone down there.

At the edge of the city the road stretched out across a grassy plain to the distant mountains. There were no farmhouses out there. Just a few sheep as grey as the Eden City skies and skinny as the beggar on the street corner.

"Got a penny for an old soldier? I lost my legs fighting for your freedom, lady!"

He wore a tattered uniform and sat on the wooden sidewalk. His legs seemed to stop at the knees.

Ma ignored his plea and told him, "We're looking for some place where we can put on a show."

"Got a penny?"

"I may have if you tell me where to find the sort of place I need," she said and began to describe it. While she talked I dropped to my knees and crawled under the sidewalk. The wooden walkway was knee high and held up on wooden pillars. I slipped under easily. What do you think I found there? The old soldier's legs!

Don't worry, they weren't chopped and rotting on the ground. They were dirty and the feet smelled but they were still fastened to the rest of his body. It was an old trick and one I'd seen before. He just cut a couple of holes in the wooden sidewalk and pushed his legs through. It *looked* as if he had no legs but really they were just hiding.

I stuck my head out and called up, "Pass me the knife, Ma!"

Ma pretended to look surprised. "The knife?" she said and pulled the long blade from the belt on her skirts. "What for, Samuel?"

"Some poor feller has his legs stuck under the sidewalk. I reckon if I cut them off I'll set him free."

"Here you are, son," she said and passed me the knife.

"No-o-o!" the old soldier wailed. "They're *my* legs... don't touch them. Aggghhhh!" he screamed as I grabbed each ankle.

"How can they be your legs?" Ma asked. "You lost yours in the war!"

"I didn't! I didn't! I didn't!" he cried.

"No, you didn't," Ma said quietly. "My little Samuel just found them for you. I guess you should offer to pay him a reward for the return of your legs, shouldn't you?"

"I never lost them!"

Ma leaned down and called to me, "Cut them off, Sam – he never lost them so he won't miss them!"[3]

"No-o-o!" I heard the soldier cry out and felt him

3 If you think about that it doesn't make sense. I know. But when someone is threatening to slice off a leg you aren't thinking about "sense". In fact even if someone was about to slice off something small like your nose or an ear, you'd still not be thinking straight. Would you?

struggle to kick free of my grip. I was as skinny as a pigeon's leg in those days but it's hard to get out of a position like that.

"So does Sam get the reward?"

"Yes! Yes! Yes!"

"All right, Sam," Ma called down and I slid out. She was emptying the beggar's hat that was full of coins and he was snivelling miserably.

"It took me hours to get that money," he sniffed.

"Ah, but what a bargain! It's a small price to pay for a pair of legs," Ma reminded him.

He thought about it. "True."

"Now you can go out and get a job!" she told him.

He wriggled his legs out of the hole. "I can!"

She jangled his coins in her purse. "Now, you were going to tell me where I can set up our show. If you do that I'll pay you a penny."

He rose to his feet and rubbed at his stiff legs, just glad to have them. "The Storm Inn on the waterfront," he told us eagerly. His pale eyes were fixed on the purse. "It has a sort of stage and they put shows on there from time to time."

Ma bowed her head. "Thank you, sir. Here is a penny. Spend it wisely."

The man's face lit up in a broken-toothed grin. "I will, lady, I will." He looked at the shining coin. "You're very kind. Generous," he said.

He ambled off happily. It would take him a while to realize she'd only paid him with his own money. I guess the shock of nearly losing your legs can do that to your brain.

We went back to the waterfront and found the Storm Inn, facing the river. We collected our cart from the sailor. Ma pulled it across the road.

The cart was creaking and the wheel wobbled like a drunken donkey. The faded letters had been painted on the side many years before. You could just make out that they read:

Jenny Wonder's Medicine Show.

We took our bags off the cart and went into the inn. It should have been lighter in here – the windows faced onto the river. But those windows were so crusted in dirt it was as dim and dark as a bottomless grave. A pair of candles on the bar lit a room filled with stained tables and broken chairs. There was a rough bar with bottles and pots behind it.

A greasy-faced man spat into a pot and wiped it. "Sorry, we're not open yet," he said. I guessed he was around forty years old and was a little bit fatter than he was tall.

"I'm looking for a room for me and my son," Ma said.

The tavern-keeper's greasy eyes slid up and down our patched and faded clothes. "You got money?"

"I put on a show. The Storm Inn will make more money from selling beer and food when there's a show on."

His face was pale as scone-dough with two currants for eyes. "I'm not paying you. You may not be any good."

Ma shook her head. "We sell Jenny Wonder's special medicine. It pays for the show. *You* lend us the stage and we *both* make money."

The man saw the sense in that and the deal was done. He even offered us a pot of ale and two plates of something he called lamb stew.

"Alice!" he called.

The door behind the bar creaked open and a girl appeared. Her skin was black and her eyes were wide and frightened. "Two ales and two stews," he told her. "Make it quick or you'll taste my belt."

The slave-girl disappeared and was back in moments with our pots and plates.

The tavern-keeper said the girl would taste his belt. It had to taste better than his stew.

I chewed it till my jaw ached. "It's a long time since this piece of gristle was a lamb," I grumbled.

"Never mind, Sam," Ma said and ruffled my hair. "This time tomorrow we'll be on our way with our pockets full of money."

"Yeah," I sighed. I'd heard it before. Sometimes we escaped with a little money but it was soon spent. Sometimes we were lucky to escape with our lives when our customers drove us out of town.

I finished the stew and wiped the plate with some bread that was just a little bit harder than the seat of my stool.

Ma slapped her hands on the table. "Time to go and make some medicine," she said.

Ma led the way to the door. She was a tall woman and well built. She could crush walnuts in her arms. In a fight she was as fierce as any man. I reckon her stare could peel paint at fifty paces. Some men said she was "handsome". To me she was the most beautiful woman in the world.

Ma strode along the street, pulling the cart, and the stray dogs ran for cover. I had to run to keep up with her.

We turned down dark, narrow lanes almost as if she knew the way. We'd never been to Eden City before – we *never* went back to a town twice.

It seemed as if Ma was following a scent and her nose never let her down.

Just when my legs were aching and I was about to beg for a ride on the cart she stopped. We stood at a heavy pair of gates. Whitewash letters said it was called:

Bluebell Bottle Factory.

We smelled the sharp tang of melted glass and heard the clatter of the bottles and glasses, vases and windowpanes being stacked. "Wait here," Ma ordered and I stood by the cart while she went inside to do a deal on the bottles we needed.

I could see a little strip of sky above my head and it was growing dark. In the alley it was already too dark to see what was brushing against my leg. It could have been a cat, a dog or a large rat. I didn't mind rats. I didn't feel too bad about eating them when it was all Ma could find. But I'd rather starve than eat a cat or a dog.

The sound of rattling glass died away as the workers finished for the day. Soon it was so quiet in the dim alley that I could hear the beating of wings. Bats, I thought.

I looked up and saw the last thing I expected to see.

A young man with wings on his back was flapping down through a gap between the wooden walls of the alley.

He landed with a soft plash in the damp earth.

He was tall and had more muscles than even Ma had. He looked at me and placed a finger to his lips. "Shush! Don't be scared," he said.

"I'm not scared of anybody!" I said.

Ma had always told me, "Never show that you're afraid. Never back off from a fight, son. Face your enemy and nine times out of ten they'll run!'

"Not scared of *any*body!" I repeated... but my voice was a squeak and I realized I was more terrified than I'd ever been in my short life.

I rested my hand on the cart and found Ma's knife on the floor. If he was going to kill me then I'd take him with me.

THREE

ANCIENT GREECE – LONG AGO

You'll remember we left the king of the gods, Zeus, trapped and helpless. He'd been kidnapped by the monstrous Typhon. The greatest warrior of the gods, Prometheus, had fled from Olympus, so he wasn't around to help. It was Zeus who had driven Prometheus out so it served him right, didn't it? Still, somebody had *to rescue him, didn't they?*

Hermes sulked. "Rescue Zeus? Me? Why me? I could get killed. I could get hurt. I could get my wings singed."

"Wor-sss-e," the snake hissed. "You could get your sss-serpent sss-sizzled!"

Hermes sighed and looked hard at the snake. "When

you hiss like that you spray spit out, did you know?"

"Sss-so what?"

"So... can you try NOT to spray it in my face?"

"Sss-sorry I'm sss-sure!" The snake sprayed. Hermes wiped his face and thought about the problem of freeing Zeus.

"I can't do this on my own," he said. "I need the boy to help me!"

He fluttered down the marble corridors of the palace and out into the gardens. He followed the sound of the music. The music stopped. There was a sound of excited female screaming. Then a new tune began. Hermes headed towards it and it led him to a fountain where an odd creature sat playing a pipe made from reeds.

He didn't look too odd in his top half, you understand. He looked like a long-haired youth who needed a shave and a haircut. A couple of short horns pushed through the hair just above his forehead. But from the waist down he had the legs and feet of a goat. The legs *definitely* needed a haircut.

This was Aegipan – but everyone called him Pan. When he was born with the goat legs, goat horns and goat beard his nurse took a look at him and ran away.

You can't blame her, really.

But Pan's ugliness had a strange power over young women.

The girls who sat at his feet and swayed to the music didn't seem to mind his strange looks. They stared at him with open mouths. Some were so open-mouthed they dribbled onto their dresses.

Hermes let the boy finish the tune. The girls squealed and clapped. "Oh, Pan!" one cried and ran up to him.

A muscular man in a black tunic stepped in her way and pushed her back. "Don't touch the artist!" he growled.

"But he's lovely!" the girl sighed. The other girls screamed and agreed. "I love him!" She jumped up and tried to look over the shoulder of the man in black. "I love you, Pan! I love you!"

She was bundled through the gate in the garden wall and could be heard sobbing. The other girls went a little quiet. The muscled guard said, "That's the end of today's show anyway."

"Ahhhh!" they sighed. The guard nodded his crop-haired head towards the wall behind them and they trooped over to the gate. "Will you be playing for us tomorrow?" one sniffled.

Pan raised a hand in farewell. "Sure. Cool. No problem. See ya!"

The man in black shooed them out, then nodded a goodbye to Pan and followed them.

Hermes turned up the corner of one lip in a sneer. "See ya? What sort of way is that for a god to talk?"

"The chicks love me, Hermes. Love my playing on the pipes. If I were in the sky you would call me a star. I am so popular, man. A popular star, that's me."

"Playing on pipes that *I* invented," Hermes reminded him sourly.

"So? What's wrong with that?"

"You love yourself even more than those girls love you. But I'm the one with the brains," Hermes said. "I invented the lyre too, you know."

"You did?"

"Yes," Hermes said proudly. "I took a tortoise and I ripped its insides out. Then I took a cow and I ripped its insides out…"

"This lyre takes a lot of ripping insides out, man," Pan said.

"Then I took the guts from the cow and stretched them over the empty tortoise shell to make strings. I *invented* the lyre. All *you* can do is play the pipes…

and not very well, if you ask me."

The goat-boy peered at Hermes. "Hey, man! You're jealous? Jealous 'cause the chicks all dig me!"

"No I'm *not*," Hermes snapped. "I have more important things to worry about than chicks... I mean *girls*."

Pan made a mock-shocked face. "You? Worry? You never worry about anything! It *must* be serious." Pan played a few trills on his pipe. Hermes snatched it off him.

"*You* will be worried when the Typhon takes over Olympus and makes you his slave."

"Stay cool, Hermes. Zeus would never allow that. Zeus would just hit the ugly bug with a thunderbolt and *pow!* End of story, you know?"

"Sadly Zeus is not going to *pow* anyone with the tendons cut out of his hands and legs. The Typhon caught Zeus before he could throw a single thunderbolt." Hermes gripped Pan by the shoulders and shook him. "Zeus is a prisoner in the Corycian cave."

The goat-boy shrugged. "So we're doomed. If Zeus can't defeat the Typhon then *we* sure can't. I guess I'll just have to keep making beautiful music till the end.

No point in worrying about it."

Hermes closed his eyes, counted to five and tried to control his temper. "If *we* can rescue *Zeus*, and give him back his tendons, then *Zeus* can save *us*."

"I'm a music maker, man!" Pan objected. "I'm not a hero. I don't even know how to use a weapon."

Hermes waved the pipes under the boy's nose. "This is your weapon."

Pan put on a stupid face and went cross-eyed. "Yeah. Right. I walk up to the Typhon and smack him in the nose with my pipe, right?"

Hermes didn't count to five this time. He simply grabbed Pan by one of his horns and dragged him into the palace. The boy squealed and yelled like one of his chick-followers but Hermes didn't let go until they reached a door with a sign that said, "Flight Room".

He pulled open the door and pushed Pan inside. "Let's find you a pair of wings," he said as he looked along a row of pegs where wings of all sizes and colours were hanging. "Here's a pair of pale blue ones."

"Where are we going?" Pan asked as he slipped the straps over his shoulders and felt the wings start to beat as he thought about flying.[4]

"The Corycian cave."

"The Corycian cave?" Pan repeated… and that was a bit of a mistake. The wings began to beat faster and spun him round so he faced east, the direction of the cave. Then they lifted him off the floor and carried him straight towards the cave. But, of course, Pan was still inside the Flight Room of the palace. He couldn't *get* straight to the cave. The east wall was in the way. The goat-boy was smashed against the marble slabs with a slap of hands and a clatter of hooves.

He fell to the floor with a groan. "I bent my horn! Oh, hell!"

The wings beat again, picked him up, then thrust him towards the floor. There was a splatter and a clatter and Pan cried out, "Why did they do that?"

Hermes hid a cruel smile. "You said 'Hell' so the wings thought that's where you wanted to go!"

---

4 Yes, that's how the Olympian wings work. You strap them on, think, "Ooooh! I want to go up in the air," and off you go. Think "Ooooh! I want to go to Athens to see the Olympic Games," and they'll take you there. But you have to be careful. If you think, "Ooooh! I want to go up in the air," and you are in a room at the time you will hit the ceiling. The wings are not THAT clever. You have to be careful. Brains splattered on a ceiling are very messy and splattered on a dining-room ceiling, they can drip into someone's dinner.

"I see," Pan said weakly.

This time the wings lifted him up and flattened him against the western wall. "What did I say?" Pan wailed.

"You said 'see'… so the wings thought you wanted to go out to sea." He reached across and pulled the straps off Pan's shoulders and said, "Maybe best if we go up on the palace roof before you do some real damage."

The two young men climbed the stairs, went out through a trapdoor onto the roof of the east tower. "Now, say Corycian Cave," Hermes ordered.

Pan took a deep breath. "Corycian Cave," he said.

The wings began to beat and lifted him steeply over the roof of the palace. The girls outside the palace gate looked up and screamed. Pan waved and sped off towards the purple mountains in the distance.

"What do we do when we get there?" he asked Hermes whose feet and helmet wings buzzed busily.

"Zeus is deep inside the cave," Hermes explained. "His sinews are wrapped in a bear's skin near the mouth of the cave where he can't get them."

"So we just have to fly down, slip the sinews back in and fly home?" Pan asked.

"It's not that easy. The Typhon has left Delphyne on

guard. She's been telling everyone who passes how Zeus is trapped. We won't be able to get near the bear skin or Zeus."

"This Delphyne is a bit of a terror, is she?"

"She's half girl, half dragon," Hermes said.

Pan threw out his arms. "No problem then! The part of her that's a chick will love me to bits. I'll play my pipes and have her eating out of my hand."

"I had a feeling you'd say that," Hermes muttered. A little louder he said, "That's why I brought you along, Pan."

"You'll slip into the cave while Delphyne is listening to my show? I like it, man. Too easy."

"Not if the Typhon comes home and catches you," Hermes said to himself. "You won't be a flying Pan, you'll be a frying Pan."[5]

The two young men soared over a forest as dark as the inside of a whale's belly. Strangled howls and screeches from hunting and hunted creatures drifted up to them. They crossed a silent desert and a grey sea

---

5 All right, that is a very bad joke but Hermes was a very bad joke-maker. He got on everyone's nerves when he tried to make jokes on Mount Olympus. His joke about the chicken that crossed the road was so bad, you wouldn't believe it. It was so bad I can't repeat it.

streaked with white, whipped waves. The sun was setting at their backs and it was turning cold now.

"There aren't any human towns round here," Pan said.

"No, the Typhon eats humans. We're getting close to his lair now," Hermes explained. "We don't want Delphyne to see us flying in. Let's land in the valley by the river and walk up to the cave tomorrow morning,"

"The river!" Pan ordered the wings.

He cried out too late, "No! No! No! I didn't mean IN the riv… glug! Glug!"

Hermes pulled the dripping pipe-player out onto the river bank. "You're lucky," he said.

Pan coughed and spat out fish-filled water. "Lucky?"

"Lucky I'm looking after your pipes," he said. "You wouldn't want them to get wet."

"But I'm soaked, man! Can't you light a fire to dry me out?"

Hermes smiled a wicked smile. "Just upset Delphyne and her dragon breath will dry you out in a moment. Heh!"

Pan shivered in the growing dark. "That's not funny."

"Yes-sss it is-sss," Hermes' snake hissed.

FOUR

EDEN CITY – 1785

Flying gods? Who'd believe that? I wouldn't… not until I met one. He landed beside me in that Eden City alley at dusk. If I were going to make up a story I wouldn't make up anything as stupid as that. So I have to be telling you the truth, don't I?

"Help me," he said. He was dressed in a cream tunic and leather sandals. He threw off his wings and held them towards me. "Hide my wings on your cart, please," he asked.

I pulled out the knife so he could see it in the fading light. "You put them in the cart," I said.

He hid them under the floor cloth. "I need some clothes," he said.

"You do look a bit odd in those. Are you some sort of actor?" I asked him.

"No. I'll explain… but it may take a while for you to believe."

I smiled. Ma and I spent our lives telling people our ditchwater was a magical medicine. Most people will believe *anything* if you tell them it's true enough times. The bigger the lie the quicker they swallow it.

"Follow me," I said and led the way to the end of the alley where I'd seen a general store. The sky was an ugly purple-red now and lanterns were being lit in the windows. But the storekeeper was too mean to light his so it was close to dark inside. Perfect.

"Buy me some clothes and I'll repay you with work," the stranger said.

"I've no money," I told him. "But I'll get you the clothes. All you have to do is keep the storekeeper talking while I slip in and out of his shop."

The man nodded. He stepped into the doorway and called in, "Excuse me?"

The owner of the shop stepped onto the sidewalk. "What do you want?" the skinny, sour-faced man asked.

"A little help, sir," the man in the tunic said. "I have a problem."

"We all have problems, sir," the storekeeper sighed. "My wife has a fever and I've no one to help in the store. I work here from eight in the morning till eight at night. You think *you* have problems?"

The man in the tunic nodded but he hadn't got the storekeeper far enough from the door for me to slip inside. "I have a thousand dollars," he said.

The little man blinked and looked at the stranger with a little more respect. Then with suspicion. "In Eden City? There are fifty people I know would kill you for a thousand dollars!"

"That's why I buried it."

"Where?"

"In the ground."

"I didn't think you'd buried it in the river. I mean where's the ground?"

"It's a secret."

The store-keeper sighed. "I thought it might be." He squinted up into the stranger's face and stepped forward. "Why are you telling me this?"

"Because I need your help."

"To get the thousand dollars?"

"To get the thousand dollars."

I slipped into a deep shadow by a bag of grain, then

squeezed behind the storekeeper's back and through into the store. The men went on talking as I searched for the clothes section.

"What help can *I* give you?"

"A spade. I need a spade to dig up the treasure."

"I can sell you one of those."

"Ah, but I have no money. I was robbed on the road. They even took my clothes!" the stranger said.

"And left you with just your shirt." I heard the storekeeper click his tongue in disgust.

I picked out some breeches that felt about the right size and a pair of stockings. I found some boots in finest leather and a wool jacket he'd need in the autumn air. I found a felt hat and finally a shirt. I crept back towards the door.

"So," the store keeper was saying, "if I give you a spade then you give me a share of your thousand dollars?"

"That's right, sir."

"How *big* a share?"

"Oh… let's say *half*, shall we?"

The little store keeper gurgled as if he were going to choke. "Five hundred dollars?"

"Not enough? Make it *six* hundred!"

"Six? Six *hundred* dollars? I'll get that spade now!"

He turned to enter the shop as I was about to leave. I threw myself to one side and landed on the floor between two barrels that smelled like gunpowder. It was so dark in there the little man couldn't see me. When I heard him pass my hiding place I collected the clothes and scuttled to the door.

I thrust the clothes at the stranger and hissed, "Run!"

"Where?"

"Back to the cart."

He nodded and his powerful legs left me way behind as he raced down the alley. "Hey! Mister! I got your spade!" a voice called in the dimness behind me. The only answer it got was the yowl of an Eden City cat.

I caught up with the stranger when I arrived at the wagon. "Where did you learn to lie like that?" I asked.

"Eden City," he laughed. "I've had some good teachers."

The stranger took the clothes and climbed into them quickly. They weren't a bad fit when you think I was shopping in the dark. He stuck the hat on his head just as the gates to the bottle factory swung open and Ma came out. She had some crates with bottles.

The stranger moved quickly to pick them up and put them on our cart.

Ma peered at him in the gloomy light of a lantern and said, "Thanks, son. I could use a strong man like you in my business. Want a job for a couple of days?"

"I may as well," the stranger said.

"You can start by pulling the cart round to our lodgings," Ma said as she placed the lantern on the front of the wagon. "We're staying at the Storm Inn," she said. "It's down by the waterfront…"

"I know where it is," the stranger said.

"I'm glad you do," Ma said as she walked alongside him and the wagon rumbled along the rutted road. "This town is like a maze. It's almost as if the town *wants* you to get lost in its twists and turns. Does that sound odd to you, stranger?"

"No," the man said. "It will get worse as it gets bigger."

"This place reminds me of an old story I read to my son Samuel here," Ma went on. "A story about a monstrous bull that lured people into its maze and killed them."

"The Minotaur," the stranger said.

Ma was pleased. "Hey! Not many people know

those old Greek legends! You heard the story?"

"No, I met the Minotaur," the stranger said.

Ma stopped for a moment. "That's a joke, is it?"

The stranger grinned in the light of the lantern. "The Minotaur is no joke, madam."

We passed the store on the corner. The storekeeper was waving a lantern and squinting up and down the street. "You seen a feller in a shirt?" he asked. "He offered me six hundred dollars for a spade!"

The stranger pulled the hat down over his eyes and walked on. Ma just looked at the little storekeeper and shook her head. "Eden City doesn't just have a crazy maze of streets. It also has more crazy people than anywhere we've ever been. Six hundred dollars for a spade? Who's going to believe that?"

"The storekeeper did," I said quietly and we plodded on. The stranger seemed to know his way, just as he said he did. We arrived at the Storm Inn tavern and shut the cart away in the stables. Then we went into the inn. We planned to stay two nights. We always stayed two nights in towns. A day to set up "Jenny Wonder's Medicine Show", a day to take the money and a day to get out.

The tavern wasn't exactly a rat hole. Rats would be

too fussy to live in a place like that. The floor was covered in sawdust. It seemed that when it got dirty the landlord just poured more sawdust on top. The tables were crusted with spilled food and rotted with the bad ale that had soaked in.

"Sorry we can't stay in a better place," Ma said.

"The whole place is twice as bad as last time I saw it," the stranger said. He took off his hat and sat at a table. We ordered the beef steaks with vegetables.

"Good evening," the landlord said and shook hands with the stranger. "I am your host Malachi Maggle. Enjoy your meal," the fat and toothless landlord grunted. He was probably toothless from trying to chew his own meat. Ma sawed a piece off the end of her steak and looked at it in the light of the candle on the table. "This horse died of old age the same as ours," she said and pushed it in her mouth.

I explained to the stranger, "Our old horse died. We can't afford another one so we pull the cart ourselves these days. It's hard work."

"That's why we need your help," Ma put in. "Where are you from, stranger?"

The man looked at us both carefully and said, "You say you've read a book of Greek legends?"

I nodded. "It's the only book we have. Ma reads it to me every night… though I know the stories by heart now."

"I'm from Olympus," the stranger said. "I'm a Greek demi-god."

Ma stopped chewing but didn't show any surprise. "Go on."

"I'm pleased we're still remembered in 1785," the man said.

"You're *remembered* by a few people who read the old books – but no one *believes* in you any more," I told him.

He looked a little sad. "I guessed that. But we really were around a few thousand years ago."

"You've been around a few thousand years?" I asked. "You aren't old enough."

"No… I travelled through time to be here. I'm escaping from an Avenger." He lowered his voice and looked around. People were too busy fighting with their food to listen to us anyway. "I am Prometheus," he said. "My friends call me Theus. I gave fire to the human race," he began.

Ma nodded. "We know that story. Zeus punished you – had you chained to a mountain. Every day an eagle came down and ripped out your liver; every night it grew back just to be ripped out again the next day."

Prometheus nodded. "The Avenger takes the form of an eagle."

"But Heracles set you free," I said. "The book doesn't say what happened to you after that."

"Zeus said he'd call off the Avenger if I could find a human being who was a true hero – a good man…"

"Or a woman," Ma put in.[6]

Prometheus frowned. "Or a woman," he agreed. "But with the Avenger on my trail the only place I could hide was in the future… I came to Eden City to look. In ten years' time there'll be a temple built here… The Temple of the Hero. I came back to 1785 to find out who this hero is. If I can find him…"

"Or her!"

"… or her… then I'll be free."

"But if the Avenger finds you first?" I asked.

"Then I will be destroyed. Snuffed out as easily as that candle flame," he said. The flame wavered weakly. A pinch of my fingers would put it out.

---

6 Ma was right. Why are heroes always men in those old stories? Ma was brave as any man I ever met.

Ma spread her hands. "Sorry, Prometheus, but we're only staying a couple of days then moving on. We can't help you much."

"Sam's already helped," he said. "The clothes will get me a start in Eden City. I'll stay here till I hunt down the hero."

"Or until the Avenger hunts *you* down," Ma said.

Theus pushed his plate away. Ma had put him off his food.

FIVE

THE CORYCIAN CAVE — A LONG TIME AGO BUT NOT QUITE AS LONG AGO AS THE LAST TIME WE WERE THERE

Of course I didn't realize just how things would work out did I? How was I to know the terror that was coming to Eden City… and the hero who would rise up to save the city? If you'd told me that night what I'm telling you next, I'd have called you a dreamer. And I should know. I'm the world's greatest dreamer. That terror had already reached Ancient Greece…

Morning broke. "I'm cold, man," Pan piped up. It had been a freezing night in the mountains and his wet goat-coat glistened with crystals of ice. Even his pipe was frozen.[7]

Hermes fluttered his wings stiffly. "I'm cold too," he said.

"Sss–so am I," the snake hissed and his spittle turned to ice flakes in the air. They tinkled down onto the frozen grass.

"Take your wings with you in case we need to get away quickly," Hermes said.

"I don't have any wings," the snake snapped.

"I wasn't talking to you, I was talking to Pan."

"Sss–sorry, I'm sss–sure!"

Tinkle! Tinkle!

Hermes led the way from the river up a winding woodland path. He stopped and looked back over the plains and the forests all the way to the sea. The morning sun was thawing the pipes and Pan blew water out of them.

They heard the dragon snoring before they saw her. They climbed the last part of the path and a bush trembled in the warm snorts from her human head.

---

7 Frozen pipes are a serious problem so don't laugh. You just try blowing down a frozen pipe. Your lips stick to the pipe and when you pull it away you take the skin with it. Very sore.

The frost on the rocks around her had melted where she had been breathing.

"A dangerous chick," Pan breathed.

"Hush!" Hermes hissed.

"Hus-sss-sh!" the snake agreed.

The winged god brought his mouth close to the goat-boy's hairy ear. "I'll make my way to the bushes at the entrance to the cave. Start playing. When you see me creep into the cave keep playing till you see me escape with Zeus. Understood?"

"We agreed all this last night, man. I'm not stupid."

"Then you put on a very good *act* of being stupid," Hermes snarled.

The dragon Delphyne snuffled in her sleep and her eyelashes fluttered as if she were about to wake. Hermes held his breath. Then he tiptoed past her scaly, bronze shoulder.[8] Delphyne's fat dragon tail blocked the mouth of the cave.

There was a small gap at the top but if he climbed over her he'd waken her. If he flew over her she'd hear the buzzing of his wings. His only hope was that Pan

8 Dragons in children's stories are usually an acute shade of green. But Hermes was there and if Hermes said Delphyne had bronze scales then the dragon had bronze scales. So stop arguing and let me get on with the story.

would get her to move. He crouched in the shadow of the bush.

Pan's music suddenly filled the morning air. The notes bounced and echoed off the mountain rocks like javelins off a hero's armour.

Delphyne opened her mouth and raised a front paw to cover a yawn.[9]

Then her paw dropped but her mouth stayed open. It wasn't a yawn now, it was a gape of surprise. "Pan?" she breathed... and turned the morning cobwebs to charred powder.

Pan lowered his pipe and raised a hand. "Hi, babe."

"Are you really, *really* Pan?" Delphyne said and shook her head in wonder.

"The one and only," the goat-boy said and grinned the boyish grin that made the girls go, "Ooooh!".

Delphyne went, "Ooooh! I am a fanatic."

"Yeah... what we call a 'fan' for short," Pan nodded.

"You must have lots of... 'fans'," the dragon gurgled.

---

9 This is, of course, the polite thing to do. If you think dragons are green you probably also think they have terrible manners. But if a dragon is well brought up, like Delphyne, then it will have good manners. A well-mannered person puts a hand in front of a yawn. You should try it some time.

"Lots," Pan nodded. "All the chicks love me."

"Chicks? Well, dragons hatch from eggs," Delphyne giggled, "so I guess that makes me a 'chick', doesn't it?"

"The biggest chick of them all!" Pan said.

Her nose wrinkled a little. "Biggest? You mean fat, don't you? You think this bronze skin makes me look fat? I'm not really. I'm big-boned!" she moaned.

"No! No! No!" Pan put in quickly. "I mean you're my *biggest* fan... my number *one* fan – or so I've heard!"

"I am! I am!"

"So I thought I'd fly up here and give you a special treat. Wake you with a tune."

"And you don't think I'm fat?"

"Quite the opposite. In fact you are so *slim* I'll bet you could get up on those *slim* hind legs and dance better than any of the other chicks!"

"I could! Play me something to dance to," Delphyne ordered, struggling to rise. "Play me something that will get me tapping my feet and dancing on this rock!"

"No problem, babe. You want rock music... you shall have rock music!"

He set off playing a fast tune and the dragon slammed her mighty foot on the rocky path outside her cave. The fat tail slid out of the cave.[10] Hermes crept round the side of the bush and into the gaping hole. Suddenly the tip of the tail began to twitch in time to the music. Hermes was almost through the door. He knew that if it struck him now it would crush him against the rocky entrance.

The fear made him struggle to catch his breath as he edged his way inside. That was when both of the dragon's feet began to crash onto the rock and the tail gave a mighty swish. It caught Hermes just as he was inside the cave.

He raised a hand to protect himself… the hand with the wand.

"Sss-suffering sss-shellfish!" the snake cried as it was struck.[11]

---

10 Yes, I KNOW Pan told her she wasn't fat. But the truth is she WAS. It was all the years of lying around in caves guarding gold and gods like Zeus. If she'd done a bit more flying around and a bit less eating sheep sandwiches she wouldn't have had a belly like jelly. Let that be a lesson to us all. Do more flying and cut down on the sheep.

11   Not many people know that this is a terrible curse in the snake world. Serpents simply don't like shellfish. If you meet an angry snake then for goodness sake don't mention mussels, don't cry out "Cockles", don't witter about winkles, call out "Crabs" and leave lobsters from your language. One boy was bitten for daring to say "Scampi" within earshot of an asp. Don't ask "Why?" Just be warned.

When the tail hit Hermes, it sent him into the cold, dark air. He tried to use his wings to save himself but he was tumbling too fast. He hit the floor on his back.

The floor was slimy – don't ask why, or "what with" – you wouldn't want to know. Hermes shot across it like a tortoise thrown onto a frozen pond.

He waited to hit the cave wall with a bone-breaking crunch. Instead he was swallowed in a bundle of thick fur that caught him like a cushion and stopped him gently.

He staggered to his feet. The mouth the cave looked a long way away – he'd been thrown ten times the length of the dancing dragon. She hadn't noticed her tail flick had caught him. He raised his rod and the snake's eyes glowed in the darkness. If you are ever in a dark place a snake with glowing eyes is a useful thing to have.

Hermes bent down to look at the furry cushion. It was made from a bundle of bear skins. The bears didn't need them any longer as they were dead and wouldn't feel the cold. Hermes unwound the roll of skin carefully. There, in the middle, lay something that looked and felt like four pieces of slimy string.

Hermes knew they were the tendons that had been cut from Zeus. He peered around the cave and walked deeper into the darkness. "Dad?" he whispered and the only answer he got was the *plish* of a drip of water from the roof. "Da–ad! Zeus?"

"Here, son," came a whisper.

Hermes hurried over to the great god who lay helpless on the slimy floor. "I've come to rescue you."

"Why did it take you so long?" Zeus asked.

Hermes stepped back. "Oh, I might have expected that. Are you grateful? No. You don't greet me with, 'Thank you my brave son, thank you!' Oh, no. I have risked my life to come here and save your miserable majesty."

"Just get me out of here or… or…"

"Or you'll blast me with a thunderbolt? Not without these tendons you won't," he said and flung them onto Zeus's chest. "Fit them yourself, fat-face."

"I would if I could but my hands won't work without them."

"Exactly!" Hermes smirked. "You *need* your son now, don't you?"

"Yes," Zeus sighed.

"So say 'Please'."

"*Please*, Hermes," Zeus said but he said it through a very tight and angry jaw.

If the two hadn't been so spiteful they may have noticed the pipe music had stopped. They may have heard the beating of wings as Pan fled back to Olympus. But they didn't notice anything.

Hermes bent down, pulled open the wounds in Zeus's legs and arms and tied the slimy strings back in place. "There you are... as good as new."

Zeus rose a little shakily. He picked up his bag of thunderbolts and slung them over his shoulder. Suddenly he reached forward and snatched at Hermes' tunic. "No, son, not as good as new. As good as *old*! The old Zeus. The one who will make you suffer for calling me a miserable majesty!"

"What?" the frightened young god cried. "Help! Pan! Help! He's hurting me!"

"Pan?" Zeus asked.

"He's outside playing his pipes to keep Delphyne out of the way."

"Idiot! You are the biggest oaf on Olympus! Clown! Bat-brained boy!" Zeus raged. "If Pan could hear you cry out for help then Delphyne could. You've put us both at risk!"

"No I haven't!" Hermes pouted.

"Oh yes he has," a voice agreed.

The great god and his son turned towards the cave entrance. The daylight was blocked by some huge shape. They didn't need daylight to make it out because its eyes glowed like golden globes.

"Satisfied?" Zeus snarled at his son. "Look who's back."

"Sorry, Dad," the winged god mumbled.

Zeus pushed him out of the way and stepped forward. "Typhon?"

"That's me."

A pair of snake heads swirled around the monster's legs, their eyes glowing. The little snake on Hermes' rod stretched forward to greet them. "Hi, fellas-sss!"

Dragon heads wriggled out from under the Typhon's arms and snapped at the rod snake. It shrank back.

Zeus's voice turned sweet as honey and smooth as olive oil. "I am so-o very sorry, but I have been having an argument with my son, Hermes."

"So I heard," the Typhon growled.

Zeus rested a hand inside his shoulder bag and walked across the floor of the cave. The golden globes watched him. "I said you have the greatest mouth in the world. You can swallow a hero whole. That's why you can never be defeated. It's your mouth that does it."

"True."

"I said you can open your mouth and it would stretch from the ceiling to the floor of this cave."

"It would," the Typhon agreed.

Hermes had seen his father's tricks before and suddenly understood. "I don't believe you," he put in.

"What?"

"I *won't* believe you… unless I see it for myself!" Hermes said.

"Hah!" the Typhon snorted. "Then watch this…"

The monster's head leant back till its upper lip touched the dripping top of the cave. Then its lower jaw began to stretch open. Hermes smelled the scent of dead heroes still stuck between the monster's rotten teeth. The jaw opened further with a creak and a sigh as the monster strained.

"Go on, Typhon!" Zeus urged it. "Nearly there…"

"Nnnng!" the Typhon groaned and then it felt its chin touch the floor.

"Well done!" Zeus cried. "And here's your reward for being so foolish!" He reached into his bag, took out a thunderbolt in each hand and threw them into the open mouth. They rushed past the monster's tonsils, down its throat and into the creature's belly.

Its jaw slapped closed. It gave a curious, "Oooof!"

sound and breathed out smoke. It reached out a massive hand to grip Zeus by the throat but the hand seemed frozen. Its belly began to glow red and the light lit up the slimy cave.

The red spot began to bubble and boil. The mighty mouth opened but all that came out was steam. The dragon heads shrivelled back into the armpits and the snakes twisted in agony as they flopped on the floor.

Slowly the red-orange glow spread through the body till the heat was almost too much to bear. The skin began to sizzle and smoke and turned to a bubbling mess.

Soon the fearful Typhon was no more than a fearful puddle on the floor.

Hermes stepped past it carefully and walked side-by-side with his father to the cave mouth.

Dragon Delphyne looked on in wonder and fear. "Well?" Zeus asked her. "Do you want the same?"

The dragon-woman's head shook dumbly.

"Sensible girl," Zeus said as he marched out into the fresh morning air. "That's what will happen to any monster that tries to take me on," he boasted.

But Zeus should not have said that, he really shouldn't. It was going to cause an awful lot of trouble.

SIX

Eden City 1785 – The Storm Inn

You must be wondering how this story of Delphyne and the Typhon, Hermes and the rescue of Zeus, ties in with my tale of Eden City. You are a very curious person aren't you? Curiosity killed the cat. I don't know how – maybe it stuck its nose in a rattlesnake's den – maybe it was curious to see what happened if it lay down under a moving wagon wheel. How would I know? Anyway, the best way to satisfy your curiosity is to wait and see . . .

Ma and I talked to Theus till late into the night. The tavern had filled with sailors and beggars, thieves and cutthroats. They drank the strong, sour beer till they fell on the floor and were dragged outside by their friends.

By midnight the place was empty of customers. The landlord Malachi Maggle went around putting out the candles… snuffing them out the way Theus would be snuffed out if the Avenger caught him.

"Have you a room with a bath?" Ma asked.

The fat landlord looked at her as if she'd spat in his ale-pot. "A bath? Who needs a bath when there's a river outside the door?" he asked.

There was no answer to that… so we made none.

"Your rooms are numbers two and three," Maggle said, yawning. "You pay for them by doing a free show tomorrow night." He threw the keys on our table and went up the stairs to his own room.

When we thought we were alone at last the door to the back kitchen opened. The black slave-girl slipped out and began to gather the pots and plates on a tray. Her arms were thin as an east wind but she seemed strong enough for the job.

"Hi!" Ma said to her.

The girl jumped and backed away. Now, Ma can be scary but that evening she was being nice because she wanted Theus to see the best of her.[12]

12 Let me tell you a secret… I think Ma saw Theus as a new husband! Of course Pa was still alive, and wouldn't be out of prison for ten years, but Ma was lonely and I reckon she liked him a lot. I was young and I was a boy – at the time this thought never entered my head. Young boys don't think their Ma can fall in love. It's only now, years later, that I see how blind I really was. Women, eh? Stranger than a five-legged frog.

The heavy tray began to shake in the girl's hands and Theus reached across quickly to steady it for her. "There's nothing to be afraid of," he said.

"What's your name?" I asked.

Her voice came like a whisper of grass. "Alice."

"Do you like working here?" Ma asked.

The girl looked around quickly to see if anyone was listening for a wrong answer. "The ostler lets me sleep in the stables," she breathed.

"That's nice," Ma nodded. "A roof over your head. A little food to eat. It's all a person needs."

"But having some family helps," I argued. "Do you have family?" I asked the girl.

Alice shook her head.

"No one to tell you stories?"

She shook her head. "Maybe Theus here can tell you a story," I said.

Alice looked towards the stairs. Maggle wouldn't be down again that night. She perched on a chair near our table and listened wide-eyed as Theus told us the story of his adventures since he'd left Olympus. It was a long story of the Avenger chasing him through time as Theus searched for a hero who would spell freedom for him.

As he reached the part where he'd flown down and met me that evening he stopped suddenly. He'd heard a sound outside on the quayside.

Demi-gods have sharper ears than humans and we'd heard nothing. He rose silently, pressed a finger to his lips and tiptoed across to the stage. He stepped up onto the platform and slipped between the curtains.

Then we heard the scratching on the sidewalk and looked towards the dirt-encrusted window by the door. The faint candle-light showed a blurred shape. It seemed as if a hook-nosed eagle was peering into the room. One glittering eye caught the light of the candle and it seemed to be staring straight at me.

I felt sick with fear.

The eagle head vanished and there was the clack of a claw against the door. *Tap! Tap! Tap!*

Alice rose to her feet and headed towards the door. "No!" Ma said.

"If it's who we think it is then a closed door won't stop it," I said. Ma looked at me and nodded.

Alice shuffled across, pulled back the bolts and let the river mist drift into the room. The mist seemed to make the outline of the figure hazy. I thought I was looking at a bent old man with a curved nose, dressed in a cloak of red-gold feathers. But sometimes I thought the mist cleared for a tiny moment and I saw a vicious bird with a beak like a curved, bronze razor.

"Sorry to disturb you," the visitor said.

"We were just going to bed," Ma told it and began to rise to her feet.

"I won't keep you long, I promise. I am looking for a man…"

"Hey," Ma laughed. "Same as me! I've been looking for a man since my husband went to jail. If you find one let me know. Ha!"

The creature stared at her. If it was laughing it didn't show. "A tall man with long dark hair and with the body of a god. I've been looking for him for a long time. There is a reward for his capture."

"You're a bounty-hunter?" I asked. "I've heard about people like you."

"You could call me that."

"So what's the reward?" Ma asked.

"Tell me where he is and I'll let you live," the creature said simply. "Lie to me and I'll kill you."

Ma is tough. But I could see that even she went pale as moonlight when he said that.

"What makes you think he's here?" I managed to

say though my mouth was dry and my throat tight as a hanged man's.

"I know he will return to Eden City someday to find who is worshipped in the Temple of the Hero," the Avenger said.[13]

"There is no Temple of the Hero," I told him.

The Avenger turned the glittering globe eyes on me and seemed to look into my heart and mind. "No, but I've been to Eden City many times and I know it will be built here soon. And I know Prometheus will return to find out who that hero is. Then I will take him, I will crush him and I will bring his worthless spirit to Hades in the Underworld."

"Good luck, stranger," Ma said. "I hope you find him. Me and Sam haven't seen nobody like a Greek god."[14]

The curved beak turned towards Alice the slave-girl and I knew we were finished. The poor child would never stand against something as powerful as

13   No, he didn't SAY he was the Avenger. He didn't have a hat with a band that said, "Say hello to the Avenger." But I guessed it and YOU must have guessed it so let's not beat about the bush or bush about the beat. Trust me it could be nobody else.

14   The clever reader will have worked out that if you HAVEN'T seen NObody it means you HAVE seen SOMEbody. Ma was telling the truth – we HAD seen somebody who looked like a Greek god. She knew it was just too risky to try lying to this monstrous bird.

the Avenger. If the bird face had had eyebrows it would have raised one of them I'm sure. "Well? Have *you* seen Prometheus?"

"I've not seen nothing, mister!" Alice said cleverly. I wanted to cross the room and hug her but that would have given away the lie. "I've seen a dog with three legs and I've seen a cloud that looks like a crocodile but I've not seen no man that looks like a god!"

The Avenger stamped its foot in the damp and filthy sawdust. "He is somewhere near," it said.

"What makes you think that?" Ma asked.

"I met a man who thinks he's seen him..." the Avenger hissed as it turned to go out of the door. "A storekeeper who says someone like Prometheus offered him a fortune for a spade."

"A spade? Who would pay six hundred dollars for a spade?" I jeered.

The creature stopped. It turned slowly and looked at me for what felt like two weeks... maybe even three. "I said nothing about six hundred dollars... how did you know how much Prometheus offered him?"

I couldn't answer. I knew why my mouth was dry – all the water had run to my knees and turned them

65

weak as rainwater. "I… I…er… I…"

"Awww!" Ma cut in. "That storekeeper's been going all around town telling everyone that story! He's loopy!"

"Loopy?" the Avenger asked.

"You know… cracked!"

"Cracked?"

"Off his chump… screwy… daffy, dappy, dippy, loony, loopy, goofy, potty, dotty. He's bird-brained!"

"Bird-brained? He must be very clever then," the bird-headed stranger said. "We bird-brains will be too clever for Prometheus, you'll see."

"Cleverer than a Greek god?" I asked carefully.

"Yes-ss," the Avenger hissed and turned back to me. "If you want to catch a rat you lay a trap. And in the trap you put some bait. The rat comes out to get the bait and then you get him! Well that's what I'll do with Prometheus. He has a weakness for those miserable humans. As soon as I threaten some of them then Prometheus will come out to rescue them. He won't be able to help himself!" The big bird may have looked like an eagle but it sounded as if it were crowing. "Then I'll have him. I'll crush him! I'll destroy him! You see if I don't."

The monstrous bird rolled on its short legs back to the door.

"Where are you going?" I called after its feathered back.

It half-turned its head to answer. "If I can't take Prometheus to Hell then I will bring Hell to Prometheus. I will make Eden City into Hell on Earth. I am the Avenger[15] ... and revenge shall be mine!" A hook of the wing threw the door open and it disappeared into the river-fog of the night. We heard its huge wings clatter and fade and disappear.

"Bird-brained," I muttered.

"But more dangerous than anything you've ever met," Theus said as he stepped out from behind the curtain.

"What will it do?" I asked.

The demi-god shook his head slowly. "I don't know. I only know that, when it starts, Eden City will be the last place you'd want to be. Get out now. Save yourselves. Leave before it's too late."

"I can't," Alice said in her soft voice.

"And I won't!" Ma said angrily.

15 I told you so, didn't I?

"Me neither," I put in. "Ma and me's afraid of nobody, isn't that right, Ma?"

"Right, son," she said and wrapped an arm around my skinny shoulders.

"We stay and fight," I said, braver than I felt inside.

Theus looked at us with wonder and respect.

"And I'll help you fight too," Alice said.

Theus shook his head and looked towards the blackness beyond the window. "Heroes," he muttered. "Where is Zeus when I have heroes to show him?"

You know the answer to that, don't you?

SEVEN

I won't describe Hermes' and Zeus's flight back to Olympus. Nothing much happened. They scared a few crows on the way — which is interesting if you're a crow reading this. But even if you are a crow you'll be saying, "Caw! Let's just get back there and see what happened next…"

Zeus landed in a rage. "Monsters! Nothing but *monsters*. Where are they all coming from? They make our lives a misery."

Hera was wrapping a bandage round Hermes' snake where its scales had been scorched by the Typhon's dragon flame. She looked up at her husband. "You've no one but yourself to blame," she said calmly.

That made Zeus even angrier. "That's right... blame *me*. Why do I *always* get the blame?"

"Maybe because it's usually your fault, dear," Hera said sweetly as she tied a neat knot in the bandage. The snake sighed.

"The world is full of monsters. It's like one of those long tales the human poets tell. Sagas. Monsters are popping up everywhere. HOW is that MY fault, I ask you?"

"Well, Dad," Hermes put in, "it was you who banished Prometheus – the only hero who would stand against them. Some people might say it serves you right!"[16]

"Then I will have to find Theus and bring him back," Zeus snapped.

Hera shook her head as she put away her bandages and potions. "You sent the Avenger after Theus. You can't call it off now. It's against the law of the gods. Theus can *earn* his freedom by doing the task you set him. Nothing else will do!"

Zeus paced up and down the marble floor of the palace. "The Avenger is just another monster. With the

16 Isn't that what I told you a few chapters or so ago? Wasn't I right? You see, even a god like Hermes agrees with me.

help of Theus I'll destroy all the rest and leave the Avenger till last."

"Then you'd better find Theus before the Avenger does," Hermes said as he patted his pet snake's head.

"I can go straight to him," Zeus told his son. "He's hiding in a place called Eden City in the year the humans call 1785. I'll go to him now. The monsters will be looking for him at Olympus."

Hera turned to her son. "If Olympus is going to be a battlefield for monsters then I'm going to Africa for a holiday," she said and hurried from the great hall. "I'm off to the Flight Room to get myself a pair of wings."

"Wait for me, Mum!" Hermes said and fluttered after her.

Zeus sat on his gold and marble throne and closed his eyes. As his wife and son looked back he seemed to fade in the soft Olympus air. Maybe there was a small "pop" as he finally vanished.

But Hera was wrong. The battlefield for monsters was going to be a long way from Olympus. A long distance and a long time away, because…

The monsters were meeting.

Imagine your worst nightmare. It was like that only

ten times worse. At the Corycian cave most of the world's monsters had gathered. Delphyne the dragon-woman sat at the back. She'd called the meeting after her friend the Typhon had been thunderbolted by Zeus but now she didn't quite know what to do.

"I don't quite know what to do!" she said to a crocodile-headed man from Egypt known to his friends as the Devourer.[17]

"Don't worry, Del girl, the brothers and sisters will take over. Just sit back and listen."

"It's exciting," Delphyne said. "I've never seen so many monsters gathered in one place before."

"We've never been in so much *danger* before," the Devourer said. "If we don't stop Zeus he'll turn us all to a blob of sticky stuff."

"Like the Typhon on the floor of my cave," Delphyne said and shuddered. "I scrubbed and scrubbed that blob but it won't shift."

The Devourer nudged her with a scaly elbow. "Don't worry, love, I know a monster who has spit

17 He got this name because he waited for the spirits of dead Egyptians in the afterlife. The spirits were tested to see if they were pure. If they failed the test then Ammit – the Devourer – swallowed them. Simple. Now don't ask me to explain why every monster has the name it has or we'll never get on with the story. Just take my word for it.

that will melt a mountain. He'll get rid of it for you after the meeting."

The dragon-woman pulled a face. "I just hope no one goes into the cave and sees it. They'll say I can't keep a nice clean cave."

"Don't worry... now, hush... the Minotaur is going to speak first."

"Brothers and sisters, you see before you a very angry monster!"

"Where?" Delphyne asked.

"On the platform," the Devourer said patiently. "He's talking about himself."

"Oh! I see!" the dragon-woman smiled.

The Minotaur had the head and tail of a bull on the body of a man. "Brothers and sisters, I am angry because we face destruction," he bellowed. "Are we going to take this lying down?"

"No-o!" most of the monsters roared back.

"Yes-s!" the Python hissed. "I take everything lying down because I can't stand up because I haven't any legs."

The rest of the monsters agreed he had a good point.

"I mean are we going to die peacefully? Are we going to let ourselves be slew by Zeus?"

"I think you'll find the word is slain," one of the beautiful Siren women pointed out. She was very good with words because she wrote so many songs to lure sailors to their deaths.

The Minotaur was getting a bit upset at the interruptions. "Are we going to let ourselves be *SLAIN* by sluice… I mean *juice*… I mean Zeus?"

"No!" the monsters cried.

"No we are not. Brothers and sisters, I propose we form a union!"

"A what? A what? A what?" Cerberus the three-headed dog said… three times.

"A union, a union, a union. We will call it Monsters In Need Of Tenderness And Understanding Really. M.I.N.O.T.A.U.R. for short."

"That's clever." Delphyne smiled.

"Hah!" the Devourer snapped. "How vain is that? Naming the union after himself?"

There was a lot of argument. In the end they decided to name the union after the Typhon whose death brought them together.

"Great name," Delphyne smiled. "Terrific Young Petrifiers Hate Olympus Nasties. T.Y.P.H.O.N…. in memory of my friend." A tear trickled down her cheek and turned to steam when it hit her fiery breath.

The monsters began to stamp and cheer and sing.

We love you TYPHON, we do.
We love you TYPHON, we do.
We love you TYPHON, we do.
Oh-hh-hh TYPHON we love you!
Oi!

The Minotaur waved a hand to bring them back to order. "Yes, brothers and sisters – remember our motto!"

"Ye-ss!" the crowd cheered. Then they stopped.

"We haven't got one, one, one," Cerberus snarled.

"We have now," the Minotaur said and he unrolled a scroll of parchment that he fastened over the mouth of the Corycian Cave. "And there it is!"

A few monsters cheered. Most of them said, "That's daft."

Cetus the sea monster said, "Monsters chew people, burn cities and even hide under children's beds. One thing they do NOT do is learn how to read!"

"That's right, right, right!" Cerberus barked. "Who ever heard of a reading dog?"

The Minotaur held up a hand. "Then I shall read it

to you... as I CAN read. It says, 'The monsters, united, shall never be defeated'."

He stamped his foot on the platform and began a chant that the others joined in. "The *mon*-sters, un-*i*-ted, shall *ne*-ver *be* de-*fea*-ted."

Over and over they chanted it, till the noise was so great the birds for miles around were shaken out of their trees.

Tentacles and talons were thrown around shoulders as the excited creatures danced in circles.[18]

At last the monsters grew tired and some had lost their voices. The Minotaur gave one last cry: "The monsters have nothing to lose but their chains. They have a world to gain. Monsters of the world, unite!"

Tired cheers faded until the Siren's soft voice was heard. "Yes, Minotaur, but what are we actually going to *do*? We can't stand here and talk. We need to do something. Something monstrous."

"Correct, Sister Siren. And we are going to march on Olympus and destroy Zeus. If we all attack at once – from the sea and the sky and the land – then he

18   It's said that the Python, being a serpent, formed itself into a circle and did its best to shake, ripple and roll... a new dance that may be very popular one day.

can't possibly kill us all with his thunderbolts, can he?"

"Are you saying he could kill some of us?" the nervous Stymphalian Birds asked.

"Some... yes," the Minotaur admitted.

"Which of us?"

"Well I don't know, do I?" he bellowed. "The monsters, united, shall never be defeated."

"But SOME of us might be defeated... and *we* don't want to be *some* of the *some*," the Stymphalian Birds chirped in and rattled their brass feathers.

A few monsters looked uncomfortable and muttered about having to go home for lunch. Then a quiet but harsh new voice spoke up. "It doesn't matter, brothers and sisters. You can go to Olympus but you won't find anyone there."

"Who's that skylark?" Delphyne asked.

"Skylark? Don't let it hear you calling it that! That's the Avenger! It takes the form of an eagle – skylark indeed!" the Minotaur muttered.

"Oooops! I beg its pardon," Delphyne giggled. "I've never been any good at bird spotting. If I do get close enough to spot one then I've usually singed its feathers off by then. And birds without feathers all look the same, don't they?"

"Delphyne?"

"Yes?"

"Shut up and listen. The Avenger is the cleverest of all monsters. It will tell us what we need to know."

"Sorry."

"Shhh!"

"Sorry!"

"Shh-hh!"

"I have been to Olympus," the Avenger was saying. "I wanted to see Zeus about the destruction of Prometheus. The servants say Zeus has already left to find Prometheus and the rest of the royal family have left the palace."

"Where's Zeus gone, gone, gone?" Cerberus the three-headed dog asked.

"He has travelled into the future because that's where Prometheus is hiding. He plans to find him and bring him back here to kill you all…" This news sent a murmur of panic round the T.Y.P.H.O.N. group.

The Avenger waited quietly for the monsters to quieten. "We can wait here to be killed… or we can go on the attack."

"Attack!" the Minotaur roared.

"Attack!" the sore-throated monsters agreed.

"Then, brothers and sisters, we need to travel forward in time to the human year they call 1785. We can only do that by flying beyond the farthest stars and turning to the right."

"It's all right for a pigeon like you. But I can't fly, fly, fly!" Cerberus argued.

"I know," the Avenger said. "That's why I collected wings when I found Olympus empty."

"Ooooh!" Delphyne muttered. "He pinched them!"

"No," her crocodile-headed neighbour said. "All property is theft."

"What does that mean?"

The Devourer shrugged. "Don't know. I read it somewhere."

The Avenger explained, "There are only a few pairs of wings, not enough for all of you. I will select the monsters who fit my plan. They will form the T.Y.P.H.O.N. Hit Squad."

"*Your* plan?" The Minotaur snarled. "You're not the leader. All monsters are equal."

The Avenger turned its eagle eyes on the bull head. "Some monsters are more equal than others. That's what I am."

The bull looked a little worried. "Well… well… *I*

want to go."

"And you shall," the Avenger said. "I also want Cetus the sea monster," it added and began to pass wings to the monsters it named. "The Sphinx... the Python... Cerberus the Dog... and Euryale."

He passed the last pair of wings to a woman who wore a bag over her head. There were eye-holes cut in the front of the bag and the tips of snake heads appeared round the edges.

"Who's she?" Delphyne asked.

"A Gorgon."

"Why is she wearing that bag over her head? Hasn't she washed her hair? Is she ashamed of it?"

"She has snakes for hair. And she has to wear that over her head because anyone who looks at her will turn to stone!"

"Ooh! Fancy!"

The Avenger turned to the crowd and said, "I've no more wings to give you but I'll need one of the Stymphalian Birds... they have their own wings."

The monsters began to drift back to their homes – some looked pleased that they didn't have to face Zeus's thunderbolts. Delphyne slipped into her cave and stuck her head out – she was hoping no one would notice the Typhon stain on the floor and make her feel ashamed. The Avenger was having a final word with the chosen T.Y.P.H.O.N. Hit Squad.

"We've a long journey ahead of us. Go home, pack some food and a change of underwear (if you are the sort of monster that wears underwear). We meet back here at 0800 hours tomorrow for the last great battle of the Greek gods! Remember, chaps, the monsters, united, will never be defeated."

And the monsters believed him.

EIGHT

EDEN CITY – THE STORM INN AGAIN, THE
MORNING AFTER LAST TIME WE WERE THERE

Like Ma said you should never show your enemy you're afraid. But there's nothing wrong with me telling you... I was terrified when I faced the Avenger in the Storm Inn. I was even more terrified at his threat to make Eden City Hell on Earth. How would he do it? I suppose you can guess his plan. But, of course, you've read the previous chapter, haven't you? I didn't know about the T.Y.P.H.O.N. Hit Squad at that time...

I woke the next morning sweating. The room was cold but I was sweating.

It was the dream, you see. I was on the plains to the west of Eden City. There was no shelter from eyes in the sky. I looked up and saw the Avenger swooping towards me.

I tried to run but my legs felt like they were stuck in treacle. I felt the sharp claws dig into my shoulders and my feet became unstuck.

I wanted to be sick as the ground fell away from me and I was hauled up into the clouds. I thought there was nothing worse than flying upwards... until the Avenger let go and I was falling downwards.

At first I seemed to be flying myself. I saw Eden City spread out below me and it looked like a map of the Minotaur maze that was in our book of legends. A maze of wooden walls and damp streets that shone like silver twisting paths.

But then I knew I couldn't fly. It didn't make sense. I had to fall... and I did. Down towards the twisted buildings that reached up like tentacles to snatch at me. The little courtyards were the monstrous mouths waiting to swallow me.

I heard the Avenger cackle and knew it was dropping me the way an eagle drops a tortoise on a rock. First it cracks open the victim and then it rips out its insides and eats it.

The tallest tentacle reached out for me and gripped

me hard by the shoulder. "Sam!" my ma said. "Sam?"

I forced my eyes to open and saw my ma standing over me.

"You were wriggling all over the bed. Were you having a dream?"

"A bad dream," I croaked.

I woke damp with sweat and shivering with fear. It set my mood for the morning.

"You've slept late," Ma said. "We need to hurry if we're going to get the show on the stage."

I changed into a dry shirt, put on my other clothes, splashed water on my face and went down into the empty bar room of the Storm Inn.

Gloom.

In fact gloooooooom!

That was the Storm Inn that morning. It seemed we'd all had troubled sleep. The Avenger got inside your head and even though it had flown back to Ancient Greece it had left something behind – the way the Storm Inn plates were after they'd been washed… a sickly smear of grease always remained.

We sat around a table eating some cheese that smelled like the landlord's socks and some bread so hard you could have sharpened it into an axe.

Alice brought a bowl of warm milk from the kitchen and we used it to dip in the bread and soften it.

"In Earth time it will take the Avenger a day to travel back to old Greece and a day to return with the trouble he promised," Theus explained. "We can expect to see him again sometime tomorrow."

"Should we get out now, Ma?" I asked.

She shrugged. "We've used the last of our money on buying the bottles. We have to fill them and sell them before we can go anywhere. We can't go west because there's just plains and then mountains out there. We can't go back east because we can't afford the ferry across the river."

"We're trapped."

Ma blew out her cheeks. "Sam, my boy, where's your fighting spirit?"

"Eh?"

"Do you mean to say you would leave these poor folk of Eden City to face the vicious Avenger? Run away like a coward while a city suffers?"

"Yes."

"You said last night you'd stay and help us fight," the black slave-girl reminded me.

It was true. I was brave enough last night. But that

dream had left me shaken and scared. "We have no weapons!" I muttered.

"We have no magic medicine," Ma reminded me, "but we sell plenty of the stuff!"

"I don't understand," I said.

"I do," said Alice, nodding. "What you haven't got you can imagine. I haven't got my freedom but I can imagine I'll have it one day."

I scowled at her. "You want me to fight the Avenger with an imaginary sword?"

"No, but you have a brain. You're clever."[19]

Theus nodded. "And sometimes it's not always the fighter with the greatest strength or the greatest weapons who wins. Sometimes it's the one with the most cunning plan."

I looked at him. "So what's our plan?"

He shook his handsome head. "I don't know. We need to see what the Avenger does and then find a way to stop him."

"We sit around here all day and all night just waiting to die?"

---

19 Of course the girl was right. I have always been pretty clever. I suppose she must have taken one look at me and said to herself, "My, what a clever person Sam Wonder is!"

"No," Ma said, finishing off her bread and milk. "We get ready for tonight's show."

And that's what we did. I took a large jug to the river and filled it with water. I stirred in a few bitter herbs and pepper to make our medicine. It would taste horrible but people will tell you: "If it's nasty it must be doing you some good!"

Theus and Ma took a painted canvas cloth out of the cart and hung it at the back of the stage then helped me fill the bottles from the jug.

It was growing dark by the time we'd stuck the last label on the last bottle. Labels that read,

Jenny Wonder's Magical Medicine.
Cures anything and everything.

People were drifting into the Storm Inn and I needed to get changed, ready for my part in the show.

First we did comical poems and songs to get the audience in a good mood, then Ma started to sell her Magical Medicine to the happy crowd.

My costume had to be made very carefully and cleverly, because halfway through the show I had to disappear out of the back of the stage, walk round and come back as a member of the audience. Why, you ask? Wait and see.

The stage was set with the painted canvas at the back. It showed a street scene with colourful houses and happy children playing outside. Rosy-cheeked girls leaned from windows to chat to rosy-cheeked lads. All in all it was meant to show you a healthy sort of place... a place that never was... but a place you wish was (if you know what I mean). Most of the happy people had bottles of *Jenny Wonder's Magical Medicine* in their hands.

We waited till eight o'clock clanged on the barroom clock. By then the bar was full of drinkers and the drinkers were full of bad beer.

Alice was hurrying from table to table collecting the empty pots and serving full ones. A few toothless customers ordered the mutton stew. (If they hadn't eaten the stew before they wouldn't have been toothless.)

I blew on a small trumpet to shut the crowd up.

Ta-raaaa!

A few people clapped. Some turned towards the stage.

"Lay-deez and gennlemen," I announced. "The Storm Inn proudly presents the famous Jenny Wonder with her famous, magical medicine show. The funniest, most entertaining show you will ever see!"[20]

We started with a few popular songs and the audience were soon joining in happily. Happy people have loose purse strings, Ma always says.

Then I did my comic poetry. You probably know it. The story about the little boy who eats and drinks too much?

But for those of you poor people who haven't seen my wonderful show I'll give you a sample here:[21]

I've just been along to the pantry
As I do, when my mother ain't near.
And while I was searching I found such a prize
Six bottles of stone ginger-beer.
Oh, I do wish that I hadn't drunk 'em
I do feel so funny inside.
My young brother said, 'Why you can't drink all that,'
Oh, I do wish that I hadn't tried.

20   It WAS the best show some of them would ever see in Eden City. For most of them it wasn't. All that mattered was we TOLD them it was a great show and they believed that what they were getting was great. People are like that.

21   It's not the same without me rolling around the stage and acting it out. But it comes into the story later so I want to prepare you. But you really, really should try to see me act it out. I am brilliant.

Inside me the gas keeps on bubblin'
I feel like a human balloon
The angels would find I don't need wings to fly
Oh, I do hope they come for me soon.

Some people were looking at the Storm Inn ale and they probably knew how the boy in the poem felt!

Then we did the act that was invented by Theus's friends, the Ancient Greeks… ventriloquism. We'd seen this back in a seaside city in the East where a man used a wooden dummy and it looked as if the dummy was talking. We didn't have a dummy. Ma just sat me on her knee and pretended I was her dummy.

The jokes weren't great but the audience laughed. You know the sort of thing…

"Say, Ma, there's a bird at the window with a yellow bill!"

"I don't care what colour the bill is, son, I'm not paying it!"

"Say, Ma, there's a pig in your bed."

"That's where it sleeps, son."

"What about the awful smell?"

"Oh, the pig'll just have to get used to it!"

Then it was time for Ma to sing another one of her

songs while I raced off to get dressed in a long coat, a hat and a false beard. I collected a walking stick from the costume box and slipped on a pair of worn old gloves. In the dim candlelight of the Storm Inn I could just about pass for an old man.

I ran through the door at the back of the stage and the cold night air slapped my face. I stumbled down the dark alley at the back of the inn and made my way round to the front.

I swung the front door open and slipped inside quietly. Ma was just reaching the time in the show when she sold the magical medicine.

"Lay-deez and gennlemen," she cried. "I hope you have enjoyed the entertainment we offered you tonight?"

Cheers.

"I hope so because I have been doing the show for fifty years now… that's right, I am seventy-five years old!"

Gasps.

"How does Jenny look so fabulous, you ask yourselves?"

Yeah.

"Well, I'll tell you… when I was a girl my old

grandpa sailed off to China and he brought back a herb they grow there. It is so rare and precious they won't let strangers buy it. He had to smuggle it out and it almost cost him his life."

Ooooh!

"Grandpa started taking this herb late in his life… so he only managed to live to a hundred and twenty. Still, it wasn't the old age that killed him – it was an accident. He was wrestling a bear in the mountains when he slipped and fell off the path onto the rocks below."

Ahhhh!

"He would even have survived that but the bear fell on top of him. Crushed him to death. But you have to agree, wrestling a bear at a hundred and twenty isn't bad going."

No.

"We managed to save a few seeds and grow the wonder plant. Every year I can make just enough medicine to fill two hundred bottles. I have them here," she said, patting the box on the table. "It will only cost you a dollar a bottle but it is so rare I insist you can ONLY buy one bottle each."

Ohhhh!

"No, sorry. One bottle each and no more. It will last you a year and I'll be back a year from now with fresh supplies. Now this may sound too good to be true but I *promise* this medicine works. In fact if you die before the age of one hundred and twenty I will give you *five times* your money back!"

That was my signal to get the money rolling. "Here, young lady!" I cried from the door. "I'm just back from the doctor. He reckons I'm so sick I have just a few days left to live. Will that magical medicine work on me?"

"I'm happy to give it a try. Step forward stranger!"

"The name's old Jake," I croaked in a voice as old as the Storm Inn mutton.

I leaned on the stick. I hobbled slowly forward and the crowd moved aside to let me through. I reached the stage and struggled to put my foot on the bottom step. Theus stepped forward, lifted me up and put me on the stage alongside Ma. The crowd fell silent.

Shhh!

Ma pulled the cork from a bottle – a bottle of clean water because I refused to drink the muck we made. She poured it into a spoon and slipped it into my mouth. I shook my head a little and leaned forward on the stick.

"How does it feel, Jake?"

"Weird… like someone has slipped some iron rods into my legs — they're so strong, like I'm ten years younger… no twenty… no, fifty!" The truth is I was probably seventy years younger than old Jake.

Awww!

"Give me the stick, Jake," Ma said softly.

"Can't do that, Jenny. I've needed this stick for twenty years. If I give you the stick I'll fall flat on my face!"

"Give me the stick."

"I'll catch him," Theus said, just the way we'd practised it.

"No!" Ma said sharply. "He will not fall! Step back, stranger!" Theus stepped back.

"Give me the stick!"

"I can't!"

"You can!"

"I can't!"

Now this could go on for a while. Some nights I let it go on too long and Ma got mad. Tonight was one of those nights.

"Give me the stick, you old goat!"

"I can't, Jenny! I'm too old to die! Life's been so

cruel to one who has walked down life's straight and crooked road and never barked up the wrong tree."

The Storm Inn crowd looked at me wondering what on earth I was talking about. But they were transfixed.

"I'm ready to meet my maker, I'm not afraid to die ... but this is such a cruel way to go and..."

"Give me the rotten stick!" Ma roared.[22] She raised a boot and kicked it clean away from under me ...

Gasp!!!

22   This is a true story, of course. But I have to admit I may have changed one or two words. So when Ma said, "Give me the rotten stick" she probably DIDN'T use the word "rotten". I seem to remember she used another word that would make your granny blush to hear it. So I won't tell you what it was in case you use it and I get the blame for teaching you bad language. Now get on with the rotten book, will you?

NINE

ANCIENT GREECE AGAIN — AND MAYBE FOR THE LAST TIME

I don't know why I was playing the fool on stage that night. Maybe I'd have been a bit more serious if I'd known what was heading our way… faster than I knew, faster than Theus guessed.

The monsters met at the Corycian cave the next morning. They were an ugly sight. Some were made more ugly by their battered and bruised bodies.

The Minotaur was once a snow-white bull. Now he had grass stains on his knees and rather a lot of mud on his back. He limped over to where the Python wriggled, trying to loosen a rather tight knot in his tail.

"What happened to you then?" the Minotaur asked the Python.

"It's those wings. I just can't get the hang of them," the monstrous snake moaned. "I said to them, 'Take me to my lair'."

"Where did they take you?"

"Malaya!"

"Bad luck."

"Then when I shouted, 'Turn around' they turned me so quickly I got my head in a loop of tail and it tightened into this knot."

"Let me help you," the Minotaur offered. "After all, we have to be united. Monsters of the world unite and all that... we have nothing to lose but our chains."

"And our knots," the Python said, struggling to help.

"Do you think we should change the motto then? 'Monsters of the world unite – we have nothing to lose but our knots'?"

"Well," the Python said, "it's better than that motto about monsters united never being defeated. I don't like that."

"Why not?"

"Well, I mean, I haven't got any feet. I've never been feeted... so I'll never be de-feeted, will I?"

The Minotaur decided it wasn't worth the trouble of explaining. He used his horn to pick at the knot and at last it came loose.

"So what happened to you?" the Python asked as the Minotaur rubbed at the mud on his white shoulders.

"Pretty much the same as you. I put the wings on and said, 'Take me home and rush it'."

"Where did you end up?"

"A hole in Russia."

"Nasty." The Python brought his head close to the Minotaur and spoke softly so the wings wouldn't hear, "You don't think the wings are a bit deaf, do you?"

"Death? Yes, they'll be the death of me too. I just hope the Avenger knows what it's doing!"

"Funny sort of monster if you ask me," the Python said.

"He doesn't make me laugh," the Minotaur snorted.

"No. I mean… peculiar. Not like the rest of us monsters. It seems so… cruel!"

The Minotaur squinted at him. "Cruel? We're monsters. We're *supposed* to be cruel. It took me *years* to learn how to be cruel. It's our job."

"Yes, but you eat the children they send to you in the maze…"

"The Labyrinth."

"Whatever you call it. They send children to your Labyrinth. You eat them... but you feel sorry for them while you're doing it, don't you?"

"A bit."

"You get a lump in your throat, don't you?"

The Minotaur shrugged. "There was one fat lad I swallowed last month... talk about a lump in the throat? He was a lump in the mouth, the throat and the belly, I can tell you. I don't think eating that much fat is good for me."

The Python looked over his shoulder to make sure no one could overhear. "The Avenger has no pity, no mercy, no feelings at all. There's a word for creatures like that."

"Pitiless?"

"Nah."

"Ruthless?"

"Nah."

"Cold-blooded?"

"Nothing wrong with being cold-blooded. All us serpents have cold blood."

"Sorry," the Minotaur said. "Is the word Malevolent? Vindictive?"

"Good words… but not the one I was thinking of."

"I give up."

"It's a simpler word altogether… I know what it is …"

"Are you going to tell me?"

"Spiteful. The Avenger is just spiteful. I mean monsters kill and destroy, burn and batter, but it's just a job. We go home at the end of the day and rest…"

"Put our feet up," the Minotaur nodded.

"Well, I've got no feet to put up," the Python reminded him. "But that Avenger *never* rests because it *enjoys* making its victims suffer. Spiteful. I almost feel sorry for that Zeus."

The Minotaur sighed. "But we've got a job to do. We have to stick together. The monsters, united, will never be defeated, and all that."

A shadow crossed the monsters. The shadow of a huge eagle. It landed at the entrance to the Corycian cave just as the dragon-woman Delphyne was trying to sweep it clean. It landed in some dust that she'd just swept into a neat pile. It rose in a choking cloud. "Look what you've done, you feathered fool!" she cried.

The Avenger turned its golden globe eyes on her.

"It was a stupid place to put a pile of dust – just where I wanted to land."

Her anger was swallowed by her fear. She backed her long tail into the cave and muttered, "Sorry, sir."

The eagle shook its feathers clean of the dust and called, "Brothers and sisters of T.Y.P.H.O.N.!"

Cetus the sea monster shuffled on his flippers into the grassy hollow in front of the cave. The Sphinx strutted on her lion legs. The Python slithered and Cerberus the dog wagged its tail. It also panted... which was a bit of a nuisance because it had rotten breath and the other monsters were just a bit disgusted.

The Minotaur stomped into place on his human legs while the Stymphalian Bird clattered down onto the grass. Finally the hideous Euryale tugged the bag firmly over her head, tucked in the odd wisp of stray snake and looked up at the Avenger.

"Brothers and sisters, we are about to set off for a place called Eden City. We know Prometheus is hiding there and we plan to lure him out, then destroy him..."

"Hang on!" the Minotaur roared. "It's Zeus we're after. It was Zeus who killed the Typhon and Zeus you told us we're going to get. We aren't bothered about Prometheus!"

The eagle eyes flickered for a moment. "Yes-s!" it hissed. "I forgot to mention that… the two gods are together. The two cousins. It makes no difference, brothers and sisters!" The creaking voice tried to sound smooth.

"No difference!" the Stymphalian Bird said and its wings trembled. "Two gods means twice the chance of us getting killed!"

The Avenger shook its head. "There are seven of you against the two – I think of you as my Magnificent Seven!"

"I like the sound of that," the Sphinx chuckled.

"Monst-ificent Seven more like," Cetus the sea monster said.

"And my plan is foolproof," the Avenger went on quickly.

"You haven't told us the plan yet," the Gorgon mumbled through the sack over her head.

"You haven't, haven't, haven't!" the three dog-heads of Cerberus barked and its bad breath almost choked the Sphinx.

The Avenger bowed its head slightly. "I was going

to tell you the plan as we flew along…"

"But if we don't like the plan we may not want to go!" the Minotaur bellowed.

"That's right!" the Monst-ificent Seven agreed.

"Brother Cetus here will swim down the river and destroy a ship or two. He will promise to wreck a ship or a house every day unless they give us a girl-child, chained to a rock, as a sort of sacrifice. The rock will be on the sea shore, just down the coast from Eden City."

The monsters thought about this for a moment. It seemed like a good Greek monster plot to them. The Avenger went on, "Prometheus will have to leave the shelter of Eden City to rescue the child – he's a hero. He won't be able to stop himself… even though he may guess it's a trap. That's when I'll get him."

"What about *Zeus*?" the Minotaur roared again.

"I expect Zeus will go with him," the Avenger replied and snapped his beak, irritated. The Minotaur was going to be trouble. Maybe it would be best to leave him in Eden City.

"What do we do?" the Python hissed. "Jump out and attack them?"

"Not all at once. We plant you on the road from

the city to the rock. You attack one at a time. Each attack will leave him a little weaker…"

"Them… leave *them* a little weaker."

"Yes-s, leave *them* a little weaker. If they *do* get to the rock and rescue the girl then I'll be leaving the Minotaur in the city to finish them off when they get back." The Avenger looked around the monstrous faces. "Now, can we all agree to go?"

"Where to?"

The Avenger gritted its beak. "We have to fly beyond the farthest stars and turn right. If we get it right we'll arrive on the plains outside Eden City shortly after Zeus. We'll look over the land and pick the best spots to attack. Then Cetus will start us off. Are you all ready?"

"These wings are a problem," the Minotaur said. "They don't always do what we want. What if we get beyond the farthest star and they get us lost? If they take us to some distant, deserted planet?"

"Ooooh! Scary, that's scary!" the Stymphalian Bird fluttered.

The Minotaur glared at him. "You're a bird. You're wearing your own wings. You don't have the problem we have."

"Oh, yes. I forgot."

"Stupid bird."

"No need to shout," the bird chirped.

"Stop arguing, brothers and sisters," the Avenger cut in. "Now, Minotaur, all you have to do is wait for me to rise into the air. Then say to your wings, 'Follow the Avenger'. They will do the rest. Can we *please* get started?"

"Will we be stopping for the toilet on the journey?" Cetus the sea monster asked.

"Will there be any trees along the way, way, way?" Cerberus the dog asked.

"Or should we go before we start?" Cetus suggested.

"What do you usually do?" the Avenger asked.

"Usually I pee in the sea – I mean, I swallow a lot of water, don't I? I need to go a lot."

The Avenger finally lost its temper. "Let us go. Let us go right *now*! Join me above the clouds and when we set off remember… don't anyone fly *behind* Cetus."

The Avenger spread its wings and blew the rest of the dust pile into Delphyne the dragon's cave. It flapped and rose into the air followed by the Stymphalian Bird. "Follow the Avenger!" the other six cried and the wings whirred into life.

They climbed towards the rising sun and crossed cities in the east. People looked up and pointed.[23] From that time forward there were legends of monsters with wings and the Chinese told stories of dragons in the sky.

They soared beyond the sun and past the farthest planets. Then off into the galaxy getting faster all the time. Somewhere beyond the farthest star the Avenger turned and headed back to Earth and the year 1785.

The Monst-ificent Seven (plus the Avenger) did not spell T.Y.P.H.O.N. for me and Theus. They spelled T.R.O.U.B.L.E!

23 We all know it is rude to point. But if you see a whacking great Python with wings and bits of lion, bull and dog beside him you're not going to keep your hand in your pockets are you? No. You are going to point. And I am not going to say to you, "Don't be rude!"

TEN

THE STORM INN — HALF A MINUTE AFTER YOU LEFT ME THERE

Hah! I was worried about Theus being attacked by the Avenger. I didn't know we were facing a small army of monsters. But if someone had told me they were on their way I wouldn't have cared. Why? Because I'm brave? No… because I was about to walk into my own big, fat problem. There was a chance I wouldn't even live to face the monster invasion. The people of Eden City would kill me first. Here's what happened…

We'd done it a hundred times before.

First the show. Then Ma tells the audience about the medicine. Then I pretend to be an old man who's cured by it. Then the crowds gather round to grab a bottle. I throw off the costume and race back to Ma's side to help her sell the bottles.

It's all noise and pushing. It's all arguing and shouting... until that night in the Storm Inn.

Ma had kicked the stick away from me. The crowd gasped. I swayed forward... steadied myself and swayed back. I spread my hands out as if I were balancing myself, then I took a step forward. Then another – a little quicker and a little bigger. Soon I was walking around the stage, then trotting, then skipping. "I'm cured!" I cried.

Double gasp!

I jumped off the stage, keeping my head down, and pushed through the crowd to the front door. "Wait till I tell my wife! I'm cured!" I cried as I ran into the misty Eden City night. "Cured! Cured! All cured!"

The doors closed behind me. I ran to the side alley, tearing off my hat. I pulled the beard loose and stuffed it inside the hat. By the time I'd reached the back door – the one that led onto the stage – I was Sam Wonder again.

I opened the door to the sound of excitement and jangling medicine bottles.

But what did I hear?

Nothing.

Silence.

The door creaked behind me. But on the stage Ma stood frozen. An old, frail woman was hobbling towards the stage. "Well?" she said. "Answer me, Jenny Wonder! Will your medicine cure me?"

Ma's mouth moved but it took a while for the words to come out. The crowd was silent, watching this scene. "I... er... of course, it depends on what's wrong with you..." Ma managed to say at last. "The Magical Medicine doesn't cure *every* single illness in the world."

The old woman reached the stage and peered up at Ma. Her grey hair was pulled back in a tight bun and her neck was as crinkled as a turkey's. "I have the same problem that old feller had that you just cured..." she said. "You got *him* to walk and skip around. I expect you can get *me* to do the same."

"That's right," someone in the crowd muttered. Other voices joined in to agree.

"It'll cost you a dollar," Ma said, stalling. Fifty pockets jangled and fifty coins were held out to pay for the medicine.

Ma turned and looked at me, her eyes wild and worried. I shrugged. I had no answer.

I looked at Theus standing at the side of the stage. He shrugged too.

The people in the tavern would see we were fakes. If we were lucky they'd throw us in the river and tell us to swim back to East River City. If we were unlucky they'd tie ropes round our necks and hang us from the mast of some ship.

A tall, heavy man pulled a pistol from his belt and pointed it at Ma. "Give Mrs Grimble the medicine," he said.

"You tell her, Smith," someone said. I guessed the man was the blacksmith for the town.

The coins and the pistol glinted in the candlelight, but the candle flames were all that were moving in the barroom. They were moving because there was a draught. The back door had swung open behind me.

I looked around and a man stood there in a cloak. His face was mostly hidden by the hood of the cloak but it seemed to glow like a sunset. "Good evening," he said softly. His voice was heard in every heart in the room. "Can I help?"

I turned my head away from the hooded man and looked across at Theus. He had a strange smile on his face as if to say, "I knew one day you'd catch me, but didn't know where or when." But somehow I knew we were saved. I don't know how I knew it. I just *felt* it.

Ma was first to recover. "Just selling Magical Medicine," she said. "Can I interest you in a bottle?" She held out one of our bottles of herb and pepper water to him. He took it in a hand that glowed like the candles. The bottle seemed to take on the glow.

"My family and I only drink nectar and eat ambrosia," he said.

Ma smiled, uncertain. "The food and drink of the gods? I always wanted to taste that!"

The man held out the glowing bottle. Ma took it from him. "Mrs Grimble needs it more than you, I think," he said. Ma nodded. She leaned forward, stretched out a hand, and passed the bottle to the old woman. Mrs Grimble pulled out the stopper and sniffed at the liquid. The golden glow of it lit her face and made her look fifty years younger.

She took a small sip and closed her eyes. She smiled. She carefully put the stopper back in the bottle and slipped it into the cloth bag she carried.

She looked around the crowd and lifted her arms above her head. She let the stick fall to the ground.

Gasp yet again!

Mrs Grimble stretched her arms wide and sighed. "Never felt better!" she told the crowd and tried a hop. Then a jump. Then hop-jump steps till she was dancing. There was no music but the crowd clapped as she whirled around the room. She headed for the door waving and laughing.

The sound of her laugh was drowned by the roar of the big man with the gun. "Hey! Give *ME* a bottle of that *Jenny Wonder's Magical Medicine*!"

He led the scramble to the stage. I ran to Ma's side to help her deal with the rush. People were throwing money at me and snatching bottles. Theus used his strength to hold people back in some sort of queue but it was madness and noise for five minutes.

By the time the last bottles were sold the barroom had emptied and we were left breathless and happy.

I looked at the man in the cloak. "Who are you?"

He gave a laugh as deep as a well.

Theus stepped towards him and stretched out a hand to pull back the hood on a shining head with curls as bright as lantern-light. "Cousin Zeus," he said. "What are you doing here?"

The lord of the gods spread his powerful hands. "I came to help you," he said. "The Avenger is seeking you and I thought I could be of some use in hiding you."

Theus stepped back. "Zeus, you never help anyone but yourself. Why are you really here?"

"To help you."

"And what do you want in return?"

I don't know if a golden-headed god can blush. But Zeus turned his gaze away from Theus and looked suddenly shy. "Perhaps you could return to Olympus and help me."

Theus nodded. "I thought there'd be a catch. What's happened?"

Theus stepped down off the stage and sat at a table. Ma, Theus and I joined him. He touched a jug of ale and poured the amber liquid into some flagons. We drank. It tasted like sparkling lemon to me with the scent of roses and the freshness of rain.[24]

Zeus leaned on his elbows. "The monsters are in revolt. They have all come together. They say they are going to attack Olympus. The gods have run away to Egypt and even Hera's gone on holiday. It's me against them."

"What did you do to deserve that?" Ma asked.

---

24 Ma told me later that hers tasted of fine French wine and honey. I guess the nectar stuff changed in your mouth to make it the most delicious thing you ever tasted.

"Sam and I have read about you and we know you can be a pretty vicious guy."

Zeus looked hurt. "I killed the Typhon – that's all! I had to do it. Now they're all out to kill me." He turned to Prometheus. "Come back to Olympus and help. Between us we can defeat them."

Theus shook his head. "I'm here because I'm hiding from the Avenger. If I go back to Olympus it'll destroy me. You know that. Even *you* can't call it off till I've found a human hero. It's part of the curse you put on me!"

Zeus sighed. "I know."

"You're on the run… like me," his cousin told him. "You're hiding."

"I am. But I can't go back to Olympus without a plan."

"You are king of the gods," I said. "You'll survive. You always do. Ma and I have read all of your adventures."

The door from the kitchen opened and Alice came in to gather the pots and wash them. She smiled at us, friendly but a little afraid of the gods at the table.[25]

25 Don't mock her. If you had a couple of great gods at YOUR table then YOU'D be nervous. If one of those gods was Zeus, with a pocket full of thunderbolts, you'd be doubly nervous!

Ma slapped the table. "It's late. Sam and I have had a hard day. We'll go off to bed. In the morning we'll work out a plan."

Zeus looked at her with respect. "You're a bit like my queen Hera."

Ma snorted. "Hera? I'm better than her! We can save Prometheus AND save Olympus."

I shook my head. "It's the nectar talking," I muttered. But deep inside I believed her.

I lay on the rough straw mattress and didn't sleep too well. I thought about the problem of getting Theus back to Olympus to defeat the monsters.

Of course I didn't know that Theus didn't have to go to Olympus to fight them. The monsters were coming to Eden City. We expected the Avenger but not its little army.

Just before dawn I finally fell asleep. I slept until late in the morning and Ma did too.

That was probably a mistake. We thought we had time before the Avenger returned. We didn't.

It seemed everyone got it wrong. The Avenger turned right at the farthest star in the universe just a little too soon. It probably planned to arrive in Eden City a little later.

In fact the T.Y.P.H.O.N. gang had already landed near Eden City while we slept.

By the time we went down to the barroom for breakfast they'd set their trap and started on their wicked plan.

We didn't know that as we chewed our way through the hard bread and sweaty cheese that the landlord served us.

"Where's Alice?" Ma asked the greasy man.

He lowered his eyes, ashamed, and pretended to be picking scraps off the filthy floor.

"Gone," he grunted. "Gone."

ELEVEN

EDEN CITY AND ROUND ABOUT IT – JUST
BEFORE WE LEFT IT LAST

*You are such a clever reader you'll have spotted the fact that
the Greek story and the 1785 story have now come together.
"Aha!" you cry. "Now we will see the point of telling this
story in that strange and confusing way! Aha!"[26] But you
will have to go back so I can explain what had been
happening while we slept. Sometimes it's hard to be a writer.*

Cetus felt good. After flying through the suns and the
planets, through the dust of dying stars, and dodging
the monstrous hailstone showers of comets, he was
back in the sea.

---

26 Of course you may be a stupid reader in which case you are still on
page one and instead of saying, "Aha!" you are saying "Uhhhh?"

"It's a bit chilly," he shivered as he slipped out of the wings and into the wind-chopped water of the northern sea. He was used to the bath-warm waters of the Greek seas. This was new and fresh and made his blood race.

The whale tail flickered on his huge body and his long neck stretched into the clear dawn air. He sped through the water making a huge white wave.

The Avenger circled over the monster's toothful head and snapped, "You are not racing in the Olympic Games, Cetus. You are here to do a task."

Cetus ignored the eagle-shape for a while as he stretched his stiff muscles and frightened fish for miles around. Finally he rolled on his back, fore-flippers in the air, and looked up at the Avenger. "Where is this place you want me to attack?"

"Follow me," the Avenger said and flapped ahead of the sea creature. They came close to the land where a cliff reared up out of the water like Cetus's head and hung over the crashing waves of the stony shore. "This is Plough Rock," the Avenger said. "This is where the people of Eden City will leave the victim for you to devour."

Cetus licked his lips with a purple tongue. "Why?"

"Why what?"

"Why don't I just go to this city and snatch someone off the harbour wall – a fisherman or a sailor?"

The Avenger circled. "I need to get Prometheus out into the open."

"It's Zeus we've come to destroy," Cetus reminded it.

"Very well," the Avenger raged. "Zeus. Zeus and Prometheus. I do not want them slipping away through the tangled streets of Eden City. The living sacrifice will be brought out here and chained to the rock. They will come and rescue her. That's when I strike."

"What about me?" Cetus asked.

"Oh, don't worry, you get to eat the girl."

"Mmmmm! Good. I haven't tasted a nice girl for ages. I like crunching on the bones best. They sort of crackle in my mouth. It makes me feel good to be a monster."

The Avenger hadn't time for Cetus's tales of the terror he had brought to the girls of Greece. "But first we have to frighten the folk of Eden City."

"Where's that?"

"It's under that dirty smoke smudge ten miles up the river."

Cetus reared up in the water and stretched his

slime-green neck. "I see it."

"It's the port they call Eden City. An evil sort of place that deserves to be destroyed. A place of greed where they love gold more than they love life. Start to ruin their city and their wealth and they will offer a life in return."

"Are they mad?" Cetus barked.

"No, they are human. We love life because we have seen the afterlife. But they no longer believe in us, Cetus. They've forgotten their gods. It's time to remind them."

Cetus surged through the clear water as the Avenger soared overhead. The eagle seemed to reach under its wing to a pocket deep inside its feathers and pulled out a roll of parchment. Then it sped into the murky air of Eden City and landed on the roof of a tall wooden warehouse by the docks. It waited. It watched.

Cetus reached the part of the river, close to the city, where the air grew thick with sour smoke and the water was greasy and stinking. He took a whale-sized breath and dived. Even with his monster eyes it was hard to see in the gloom of the grimy water. Then his head brushed the bottom of a barge and he knew it was time to rise to the surface.

The ugly head broke through the water close to the dock where several fine sailing ships were tied. Workers were unloading the cargoes and carrying them to the warehouse where the Avenger watched.

"Wheeee!" Cetus cried.

Workers turned, dropped their loads and fled to the shelter of the shadows by the buildings.

"Wheeee!" the monster said and shook seaweed and sludge from his hairless head.

The Avenger stretched its twisted neck forward and hissed, "Not 'Wheeee' – that wouldn't terrify a turnip. Try, 'Raaaarrrrgh!' like a real roar."

"It's a while since I've done this," Cetus sniffed. "I'm a bit out of practice." He opened his mighty mouth and tried again, "Waaaah!"

"No. Raaaarrrrgh!"

"Er… 'Rah!'"

"Oh, never mind. Just eat a ship."

"I don't eat ships. I'm a people-eater. And I'm a fussy eater. I prefer tender girls."

"Very well, just pick a ship up in your mouth, crunch it and spit it out, but for goodness sake get *on* with it!"

Cetus made for a tea trader from India. He placed his snout under it and flipped it into the air. Before it landed back in the water he caught it in his mouth, split it open with a single bite, then let the shattered timbers fall back into the harbour. The tea was scattered and stained the water. If it had been warmed up with sugar and milk it might have tasted quite pleasant.

"What now?" Cetus asked, spitting splinters from between his teeth.

"Go away and lurk off the coast. Swim up and down so they can see you," the Avenger ordered.

Cetus nodded. He took one last look at the cowering, half-hidden humans and roared, "Raaaarrrrgh... hey, that's better! I'm getting the hang of this!"

He swam back into the river and a little way out to sea where the water was fresher. He could see Plough Rock in the distance and his hunger was sharp as a knife.

The fishermen and sailors, the porters and the beggars, the ostlers and the fishwives, the children and the grannies crept out from their crannies by the docks. They looked at the wreckage in the water. They looked through the smoke of the Eden City air towards the sea monster in the distance.

No, they hadn't dreamed it.

The Avenger flapped into the air, climbed and then

closed its wings. It dived like a falling tea-chest towards the crowd on the quayside. When it was just above their cowering heads it opened its wings again and dropped the scroll onto the damp cobbles before heading off towards the coast.

A sailor picked up the scroll and looked at it. He passed it to old Mrs Grimble (who had drunk the nectar last night and could now read). She shook her head with horror.

By now half of Eden City seemed to have gathered on the quayside after the story scuttled through the streets like a rat with its tail on fire.[27] Malachi Maggle from the Storm Inn was there to buy bruised vegetables and scraps of maggoty meat for his stews. "Read it, Mrs Grimble," he ordered. He tried to lift her onto a box of cloth that had landed on the edge of the water so everyone could see her. She shook his hand away. "Get your grubby hands off, Malachi Maggle. I can climb up on my own – now I'm a very nimble Grimble."

She scowled at the crowd like a teacher waiting for her class to listen.

"It says this," she creaked and read the scroll.

27 You are correct. Ma and I were not there. We had slept late and missed everything. If we had been there we couldn't have stopped Cetus, but we might have stopped what happened next.

Dear People of Eden City,

You have seen the power of Cetus.

He is your worst enemy and your best friend.

Treat him like a friend and he will protect Eden City.

Treat him as an enemy and he will destroy your ships one by one.

Here is what you must do to make him your friend.

Take a fresh, young maiden from your city.

Take her to the place called Plough Rock.

Chain her to the cliff there.

Leave her.

Signed,

The Avenger

The crowd muttered among themselves for a while. Then Maggle pushed the old woman off the box and called out, "What are we going to do? Are we going to bow down to this monster? Or are we going to stand up and fight?"

"Well *I'm* not!" someone shouted back.

"Are we going to sacrifice one of our girls to this ravening creature, chain her to the rock and leave her to die in terror?"

"Yes!" a few more people shouted back.

"Are we good folk of Eden City such cowards that we would let an innocent child die to feed that monster?"

"Ye-es!" everyone roared back.

"All right." Maggle shrugged. "In that case we have to decide *who* is to be the victim. Does anyone have a daughter they don't want?"

One man put his hand up but his wife slapped it down. "Don't be stupid. Who'll clean the pigs if you feed our Mary to the monster?"

"Look," Maggle sighed. "It's no use agreeing to feed the thing if we can't find a girl!"

"Here, Maggle," old Mrs Grimble said. "You have a slave-girl."

"Alice?"

"Yes, Alice. No one will miss her. No one will cry for her if she goes!"

"Who'll clean my tavern?" Maggle asked angrily.

"No one cleans it *now* by the look of it!" someone shouted and the crowd laughed.

"We'll pay you gold," the old woman said. She turned to the crowd. "We'll all give something to save our city, won't we?"

"Suppose so," the crowd grumbled and pulled out

purses. Soon a bundle of money was gathered in a cloth and held out for Maggle.

"Oh, very well," he said. "You can take Alice," he agreed.

Some of the men got together to make the plans. The blacksmith would give the chains and lend one of his travelling wagons to carry them to Plough Rock.

The doctor agreed to give her a drug so the slave-girl would be too sleepy to know what was happening.[28]

The rest was easy. Maggle called Alice from the kitchen of the Storm Inn into the yard. She had been preparing our breakfasts.

As she stepped outside the blacksmith grabbed her and fastened steel bands round her skinny wrists.

The old woman fed her a drink of ale with the drug and Maggle threw her onto the blacksmith's cluttered wagon.

The wagon wound its way round the twisted streets of Eden City and out towards the ocean road.

---

28 That was kind of them, wasn't it? If you are ever faced with a flesh-eating monster who is out to make you his meal, then ask the doctor for a drug. You will probably doze a bit, think the monster is a nightmare… until you hear your ribs crack and your body burst. Then you will wake up dead. Those kind, kind people of Eden City knew that.

A few of the good folk stood in their doorways to watch. Some looked out from behind their grey curtains. Some managed to look a little ashamed… but not many… and not *very* ashamed.

The wagon rattled out onto the road. Over a river, through a forest and over a ridge of hills where caves looked down on them like dark, blind eyes.

But the river, the forest and the caves were not blind – monster eyes watched the little procession as it made its way to Plough Rock. Eyes of monsters that had been told by the Avenger, "Do not attack them. Let them take the girl. Let them return to Eden City. It is the rescuers – Zeus and Prometheus – that we want. Agreed?"

"Not even a nibble of fresh flesh?" the Minotaur asked hungrily.

The Avenger looked at the bull head. "You can stay in Eden City… just in case the rescuers *do* return. It is all part of the plan. Remember, brothers and sisters… the monsters, united, will never be defeated."

Cerberus nodded his three heads… the others nodded one each.

The trap was set and the bait called Alice was on her way.

TWELVE

EDEN CITY AND ROUND ABOUT IT – JUST
AFTER THE LAST CHAPTER AND AT THE END
OF THE CHAPTER BEFORE

It's not easy being a writer in a story where two things happened at the same time in different places. In fact with the monsters lying in wait, with Alice on her way to Plough Rock, with Maggle returning to the Storm Inn and with us coming down to breakfast there were FOUR things happening in the same story. But don't worry. They have all been tied together now like the knot in your shoelace.

"Where's Alice?" Ma asked Maggle.

He lowered his eyes, ashamed, and pretended to be picking scraps off the filthy floor.

"Gone," he grunted. "Gone."

Zeus and Theus joined us in the barroom and between us we dragged the story from him.

"You sent a girl to her death," Ma said.

"A horrible death," I added. "In the mouth of a monster."

Maggle twisted his hands and said, "She's only a slave and a girl."

I felt Ma swell with anger beside me. "Only?"

"Well, women aren't as useful as men, are they?" he asked.

"Any woman is worth TEN of you, Maggot," she sneered.

"The name is Maggle," he answered. His breathing was short and he was getting angry. "At least I provide a service for the people of the city. You just sell them fake medicine then run away – I *know* what you do. And when I tell them they'll probably come and get their money back... before they hang you! We had to send *one* girl so *hundreds* of people can be saved from the monsters."

"Monsters?" I said. "What monsters? There's only that sea monster."

He pulled back his lips to show his gums. "No, *boy*!" he spat. "A traveller from the coast saw something in the cave on the way in from the ocean road this morning. A monstrous woman with a sack over her head."

"A Gorgon!" Theus muttered.

"Probably Euryale," Zeus nodded.

"There was a brass-feathered bird in the forest and a serpent in the river, the traveller said. The sea monster isn't alone. We can't fight them all. We're not heroes," he snarled.

He rose from the table and sent his stool falling with a clatter. "Don't try to tell me you're some sort of saint, Mrs Wonder… or whatever your real name is. We all do what we have to do to stay alive," he panted. "And if that means sacrificing one useless slave to save a city then that's what we have to do."

He turned and crashed through his kitchen door.

Ma grabbed a breakfast knife and began to rise to go after him. Zeus reached out a hand and held her back. "Mrs Wonder, it's not his fault. It's my fault. The monsters are here looking for me."

Theus shook his head. "But I think they've been brought here by the Avenger to destroy *me*. It's my fault," he said. "I have to go and save the girl."

"That's probably what the Avenger wants," I told

him. "As soon as you stick your nose outside Eden City it'll pounce. You won't save Alice – you'll just sacrifice yourself as well."

"Sam's right," Zeus said. "I ran from Olympus to flee from a fight. Sooner or later I have to slay the monsters – here or in Greece. It may as well be here."

Theus buried his face in his hands and looked in agony. "Do I have to stay here while you go out there and fight?"

Zeus nodded. "Yes, cousin."

"But how can you defeat Cetus?"

Zeus shook his golden head and spread his mighty hands. "I don't know."

"I do," I said.

They looked at me. "You do?"

"Of course. I've heard the legends every night from Ma's book. We're thousands of years ahead of your age, remember. Your battles have already been fought and won. It's there, in the book!" I told the gods and Ma took the little leather-bound legends from her pocket.

Zeus shook his head, "And how do I beat Cetus and save the girl?"

"Easy," Ma said. "As you know the Gorgon is hideously ugly. Anyone who looks at her face is turned to stone. The Avenger made the mistake of bringing the Gorgon to the caves in the hills. All *you* have to do is cut her head off, show it to Cetus and Cetus will be turned to stone!"

Theus smiled gently. "And does the book tell us how to cut off the Gorgon's head without US being turned to stone?"

"Oh, yes," I nodded. I hadn't thought of that. Zeus crinkled his mighty brow. "We don't know *all* the monsters the Avenger has brought with him. What if there's a monster out there I don't know how to defeat?" he asked.

I spread my hands. "I'll just have to go with you," I said.

"You might die," Ma cried.

"If we stay in Eden City and do nothing we'll all die *anyway*," I told her. "We have to try."

Ma began to argue but Zeus was on his feet and pacing the floor. "Mrs Wonder, I'm afraid Sam is right. With my power and his knowledge we might just defeat the monsters. But we can't waste time squabbling."

"I don't let any man tell me what to do," Ma said angrily.

"I'm not a man, I'm a god!" he replied. "You are worse than my wife Hera. Another stubborn woman."

"Another *poor* woman," Ma snorted.

"Poor?"

"Yes… poor woman, married to a stupid man like you! I feel sorry for her."

"And I feel sorry for the man who married you," Zeus roared back.

"He's in jail," Ma raged.

"Then he's probably glad of the peace and quiet," Zeus jeered.

Ma picked up a tankard from the table and threw the ale in the great god's face. He blinked. He ran his tongue over the dripping liquid. "It tastes disgusting!" he moaned.

Theus stood between them. "It will only take Cetus moments to swallow a girl like that. He always eats at sunset. You are wasting a hundred moments with your silly squabbles, cousin," he said urgently.

Zeus wiped his face with the back of his hand. "She started it. She called me a man… and a stupid man at that."

"Sorry!" Ma said. "I should not have called you a stupid man."

"Thank you."

"I should have called you a stupid god."

Theus stepped between them again. "Cousin… go now!" he urged.

Zeus pivoted on his heel and marched towards the back door of the Storm Inn. He turned. "I'll deal with that Wonder woman when I get back."

"Ha!" Ma laughed. "*If* you get back."

Ma wrapped a strong arm around my shoulder and hugged me. "I suppose it's no use telling you to be careful."

"No, Ma. I'll just remember your best advice." I closed my eyes and recited it. "Never show that you're afraid. Never back off from a fight. Face your enemy and nine times out of ten they'll run."

She wiped away a rare tear. "I taught you well, son. Go out and be a hero."

I went.

It took some time for us to find our way out of the maze of Eden City streets and onto the coast road. Zeus in his cloak passed for a traveller. I had to trot to keep up with him at times.

When we left the last crooked building and

stepped onto the track across the plain Zeus stopped and pointed up to the sky. I saw an eagle circling lazily in the morning sun. It was too far away from me to see the golden eyes but I knew they were fixed on us.

"We were right to leave Theus behind. This would be the perfect place for the Avenger to snatch him."

The next time I looked up the eagle was a blur of feathers speeding down towards us. Zeus rested a hand in the bag that carried his thunderbolts and stopped in the middle of the empty road. The eagle landed and blocked our way forward. When it was on the ground it looked more like a hooded and bent old man than a bird. The eagle face was half-human. But those glittering eyes still looked like that same cold fire.

"Good day," Zeus said.

"It will not be a good day for you, Zeus. There are monsters waiting for you along your path."

"Really," the king of the gods said calmly. "Which monsters would they be?"

The Avenger hissed, "I would be foolish to tell you that. I will only say that they are a Magnificent Seven desperate to destroy you. And you cannot beat them all. It would be far better to turn back now. Go and send Prometheus out. He's a true hero. He has a far better chance of saving the girl than you ever would."

Zeus half turned to return to the city. Then he stopped. "Sorry, but the trouble is I don't know where to find cousin Theus! He may be back in Greece fighting the monsters you left behind. Wouldn't that be clever of us? First we divide the monsters into two groups – Theus kills the Greek ones and I kill your Magnificent Seven! The monsters, united, will never be defeated... but the monsters split between the two worlds could be weak as your neck."

For the first time I saw the Avenger uncertain. "Prometheus would never dare return to Greece."

"Why not? If you are *here* then he'd be safe *there*."

The eagle feet shuffled on the road. "This is the place where they will build a Temple to the Hero. *This* is the place he *must* come back to."

"We'll see," the king of the gods grinned.

"*You* won't see. The monsters will destroy you before the day is out," the bird snapped. "And I will take you to Hades in the Underworld."

"That's kind of you," Zeus said. "But they won't destroy me so long as I stand here chatting to you. If you would care to flap aside we'll be on our way."

The eagle's eyes glared for a long moment before it

shuffled across to let us through. Then it clattered its wings and rose into the air.

The road stretched through the yellowing grass to the distant hills. "There's only one way through the hills," I said. "One of them will be waiting for us at the pass."

Zeus gripped the glittering sword beneath his cloak. "We'll be ready for it."

But the first thing we saw wasn't a monster from Greece.

It was a wagon pulled by a horse. Two very human people sat on it.

One was a smoke-blackened man with muscles like Theus. It was the blacksmith. He had a small charcoal burner in the back of the wagon. I guessed he'd just used it to forge Alice's chain to the top of Plough Rock.

The other passenger was the old woman we'd cured last night, Mrs Grimble.

The wagon stopped and the blacksmith jumped down. He grabbed a poker that was still glowing from the burner and waved it like a sword.

"Where are you going?" he asked.

"Plough Rock," I said. "To rescue Alice."

"You can't do that," the old woman squawked. "She has to die to save the city."

"No! Once the monster's eaten her then he'll be back for more," I shouted to her.

"You'll be too late anyway," she said.

"Not if we have a horse and wagon to get us there," Zeus said and stepped forward. "I think we'll take yours."

The smith was a big man but quick. He took one step towards Zeus and thrust the red-hot poker straight into the god's chest.

THIRTEEN

THE OCEAN ROAD FROM EDEN CITY

Sorry if I stopped my last chapter just when it became so exciting. But I needed to catch my breath. At the time it happened I'll swear my heart stopped. Just the memory of it makes my blood freeze with fear so I can hardly hold my pen. But now that I've had a cup of tea I feel I can carry on ...

Zeus was the master shape-shifter. He could make himself into a swan or a bull, or any creature from aardvark to zebra.

At the moment the blacksmith attacked him with the hot poker he changed himself into a dragon. The poker was thrust towards his chest – the chest became the dragon's mouth. And if a dragon's mouth can breathe out fire then it can just as easily swallow fire.

The dragon jaws snapped around the poker and tugged it from the smith's hand. It threw it into the air, spinning and sparking, then caught it by the handle. In a moment the dull red end was pointing back towards Zeus's attacker. The dragon's head changed back into Zeus's hand and Zeus stood there smiling.[29]

The smith turned pale under the soot on his face. "So, now you kill us and take the wagon anyway," he sighed.

"No!" old Mrs Grimble cried. "I'm too old to die!"

"You're never too old to die," Zeus said.

"Don't kill them, Zeus," I said, tugging at his arm.

"Why not? They would kill you if the poker was in their hands. They would see the slave-girl die."

"Let them go back to Eden City and tell the people why we're doing this!" I told him.

Zeus looked puzzled. "Why *are* we doing this?"

"Because it's what Ma told me... 'Never show that you're afraid. Never back off from a fight. Face your enemy and nine times out of ten they'll run.' We have

29 All this happened a lot quicker than it takes for me to describe it, of course. It happened in a blink of an eye. So go ahead and blink your eye. Have you done it? See? That was quick wasn't it?

to show the folk of Eden City it's true!" I said, still clinging to his arm.

Zeus shook his head. "You humans are strange creatures. Showing mercy to your enemies? How could you ever survive so long on earth?"

But he thrust the poker back into the burner and said, "Do what the boy says. Go back to Eden City and tell them it's better to live like a hero than die like a coward."

Mrs Grimble began to jabber some sort of thanks for his sparing her life and the blacksmith fell to his knees like a servant before his lord. But Zeus was already turning the wagon and I jumped onto the back.

The horse trotted on and I was jolted like a flea on the back of a racing rat. I didn't mind if it meant we got to Alice quicker.

The road ahead dipped. Boulders rose on either side. There was just enough room to squeeze the wagon through and there was no way round. If the monsters were going to stop us then this would be a good place.

Sure enough I heard the hideously hollow sound of barking and looked up to see a huge dog with three heads blocking the way. "Cerberus," I breathed. "The dog that guards the gates of the Underworld."

"Stop! Stop! Stop!" the heads barked.

"Sit!" Zeus snapped back and the dog sat.

He jumped back to his feet at once. "Here! Here! Here! Who do you think you're telling to sit, sit, sit? I am Cerberus the guardian of the gates and you shall not pass."

"Well, you're not guarding the gates now," Zeus muttered.

I ran up to Zeus and whispered, "A girl called Psyche gave him sweet cakes to eat and he let her pass! Try it. It might work!"

Zeus nodded, then pushed me back.

"Will you not let us pass? Not even for a biscuit?" Zeus said slyly as he slipped the sword loose from his belt but kept it hidden under his cloak.

"What sort of biscuit, biscuit, biscuit?" the heads asked and slaver dripped to the ground, killing the grass.

"What sort do you like?" Zeus asked, edging closer.

"It would have to be three biscuits, biscuits, biscuits," Cerberus said.

"Why?" I asked to take his gaze away from Zeus. "You only have one stomach to feed."

"Ah, but we want our three mouths to taste the sweetness of the honey and the ginger… three sets of teeth to enjoy the crunch, crunch, crunch!"

"Then have a taste of this!" Zeus roared and swept the sword from under his cloak. It flashed in the morning sun and swept towards the left-hand neck of the beast. It was a firm stroke and a fine shot. The neck was cut clean through. The left-hand head leapt in the air and went bouncing off the boulders.

"Ow! Ow!" Cerberus cried.[30]

The neck wound bubbled and boiled with red froth. Two black lumps pushed up through the neck and in moments they had grown into two new heads where one had been before.

Four heads snapped and snarled at us. The dog's tail whipped round and it had the head of a spitting snake on the end. Zeus swung his sword at the snake and it fell writhing to the path but was replaced by two

30 Of course it could have been "Bow! Wow!" and not "Ow! Ow" but I was too busy dodging the spray of poisoned blood to listen carefully or to say, "Excuse me, but would you repeat that, please? If I live to write a book I want to be sure I heard you correctly."

snake heads. He cut off the right head and two more appeared. Now we faced a five-headed dog – a very angry five-headed dog.

Zeus raised his sword again. "No!" I cried and pulled him back towards the cart. "The more you cut the more will grow. He'll have fifty heads in no time!"

"Then we can't beat him?" Zeus asked.

"There is a way," I said and I thumbed through the book of legends Ma had given me. Then I found the answer. "Here… look. Blow on the charcoal of the fire!"

Zeus blew so hard he frightened the horse but the fire glowed white-hot and I pushed the blacksmith's poker into the heart.

I looked over my shoulder. Cerberus was still standing between the boulders, scratching an ear with a back leg. He couldn't attack because then he'd leave room for us to get through.

When I was sure the poker was hot enough I told Zeus, "Wait till I've climbed to the boulder over the dog's head."

"Which head?" he asked.

"Oh… all of them… it doesn't matter. When I tell you I want you to cut off a head."

"But…"

"Don't argue, Zeus! Every moment we waste puts Alice's life in danger. There may be other horrors waiting for us before we even get to her."

He sighed. "This is worse than being back at Olympus. My wife Hera speaks to me like that. Treats me like some kind of idiot," the great god grumbled.

"I wonder why?" I sighed and pulled the white-hot poker from the fire. I held it well away from me as I struggled to climb the boulder without sticking it in my eye or up my nose. At last I was on top of the rough rock and looking down on the five heads.

The nearest heads, the new left-hand pair, looked up at me and snarled. "You can't win, boy-child."

"We can. And when we do you'll never go for walkies ever again." Then I called down to Zeus, "Now!"

He swung the sword and the nearest head sprang off. The neck bubbled and a black lump appeared. Before it could grow I ran the poker over the wound and sealed it closed. The heads could only grow through living flesh, not cooked meat.

"Back to four heads," I said. "Ready, Zeus?"

"Ready!"

"Again!"

And again the sword swung, a head flew, and I sealed the neck. "Back to three – again!"

The dog was down to two heads in a moment but the poker was cooling. I wasn't sure if it would work a fourth time.

Cerberus backed away a little. "You see?" I called down. "We *can* beat you!"

The two heads looked at one another. "The monsters, united, shall never be defeated, defeated!"

"But you're not united," I said. "The Avenger has left you to fight alone. And the monsters alone *shall* be defeated – one at a time."

"The Avenger doesn't care about *you*," Zeus said. "It's Prometheus it's after."

"The Avenger won't be pleased when it finds I've let you pass," Cerberus sighed.

"No," I told him. "You'll really be in the dog house."

Zeus waved his blood-dripping sword under the dog's left nose. "You are just bait in the Avenger's trap like a worm on the end of a fishing line."

"A worm, worm?" Cerberus said. "Am I really?"

"Yes," I told him. "Zeus here will kill you if you

don't stand aside. He'll chop you up till you are a blood hound – but more blood than hound."

"Go back to the Underworld," Zeus said. "Stop the dead souls escaping. That's your job. You don't belong up here. The sun hurts your eyes."

"It does," the dog whined.

Cerberus gathered a pair of wings that were tucked behind the boulder and slipped them on his back. "Before you go… will you cut off one of my heads and let it grow?" he asked.

Zeus nodded.

"Why?" I asked.

"Because I am the three-headed dog – guardian of the gates. People will laugh at me if I go back with just two heads, won't they? 'Where's your head?' they'll ask. 'Lost it in a game of fetch, did you?' they'll say. A good guard dog has to have three heads."

"Oh, very well, come here," Zeus said. "Sit!"

Swish.

One head grew to two and Cerberus was back with three heads. "Now I'm happy as a dog with two tails," he sighed.

"You DO have two tails," I reminded him.

"So I have!" he cried.

"Now let us pass."

The dog sat there. "What now?"

"You promised me a biscuit," he whined.

"Only if you were a good boy."

"But I was, was, was a good boy!"

"You tried to KILL us!" I cried.

"I was only doing what I was told," he growled.

"And now I'm telling you to get back to Ancient Greece and the Underworld where you belong," I said.

The heads nodded and the dog strolled out onto the plain before flapping his wings and sailing off beyond the clouds.

"Ohhhh!" I groaned as I slid down from the boulder and put the poker back in its burner.

Zeus cleaned his sword on some dry grass and took the reins of the wagon. We set off at a fast trot towards a dark forest at the foot of the hills. The air was still now and it seemed as if something was waiting for us inside the forest. I yawned and stretched. Zeus asked, "What's wrong? We've only just set out."

"I know."

"And you're weary already?"

"Worse than that," I said. "I'm dog tired."

FOURTEEN

THE DARKEST FOREST YOU EVER SAW — NOT FAR
FROM EDEN CITY

*Do you like dogs? Did you want Cerberus to escape? Well,
I'm sorry, but things can't always work out the way you
want them. Cerberus may have flown home to Ancient
Greece... without his biscuit... but not every monster can
have a happy ending. Sooner or later, if you are a monster-
lover, you are going to need a big handkerchief to dry your
eyes. You've been warned...*

The river was on our left as we rattled down the road.
It sparkled in the sunlight, so it must have been a fine
day out on the water.

To our right the golden prairie grass rippled in a
friendly breeze and small cloud shadows chased each

other all the way to the mountains.

Eden City, behind us, was covered in a woolly carpet of smoke – but that was from the crude coal they burned in their fireplaces and factories.

Ahead of us there was just gloom. It wasn't smoke like the fog around Eden City. It was as if the purple murk of the forest was spreading upwards to blot out the sunlight. There were no singing birds and even the sounds were swallowed up.

It was that sort of forest that you hear about in fairy tales. If Hansel and Gretel had come running out of a gingerbread cottage I wouldn't have been surprised. [31]

The path ran straight into the forest. The trees stretched to the river on the left and a long way to the right. It would take hours to try to go round the outside. The horse slowed down as if it sensed danger. Zeus had to jump down and lead it by the reins. Sometimes it dug its hooves into the damp turf and the god had to use his great strength to drag it along.

We'd only gone a short way when the light behind

---

31 Well, I WOULD have been surprised because, as you know, fairy tales are not true. The legends of the Greek gods and their monster enemies are true – I know, I've met them. But Babes in the Wood, the Three Bears, Jack and the Beanstalk and those sort of tales are just made up… I think.

us disappeared. Then we turned a corner and the light above us faded as the branches above seemed to join together over our heads.

"It's like the houses in Eden City," I said. "The way they come together over your head and make daytime into night."

Zeus was treading carefully now. With his free hand he held a sword as dull as lead in the dead light.

In the back of the cart the charcoal fire glowed. I jumped to the ground, picked up a branch that was sticky with sap and thrust it into the burner.

The branch spat and sparkled into life and gave us a sort of light. We reached a crossroads. There was a signpost there. I raised the branch like a torch and read it. The right arm said, "Plough Rock", the road ahead said, "Eden City", the left arm said simply, "Death". The way we'd come said, "Destruction".

Zeus tugged the horse's head to the right.

"Where are you going?" I asked.

"Plough Rock," he said softly.

"No!"

He stopped. The horse snickered softly. "It's a trick," I said.

"So which one do we take?" Zeus asked.

"I don't know," I told him. I needed to think about it.

I took the poker and scorched the crossroads on a piece of bark that lay on the ground. I wrote the names Eden City, Plough Rock, Death and Destruction on the way the signpost said.

"Eden City is where we've just come from," I said. "So that needs to be pointing backwards."

"Hurry," Zeus urged.

"No point in hurrying," I told him. "If we get it wrong we won't get there anyway."

I turned the bark map so Eden City pointed back the way we'd come. "Now the map says we need to turn left for Plough Rock."

Zeus turned his great golden eyes on me. "But the signpost says that way leads to Death."

"I know."

"The signpost is lying?"

"Yes."

He turned the horse and began to lead it towards the road marked Death. "Are you sure?" he asked.

"No," I murmured.

Zeus laughed. "You're a brave one. Maybe Prometheus is right. Maybe there is a hero amongst you humans after all."

"Then it's not me," I told him. "I'm shaking."

"But you are still going forward. That's courage," Zeus said.

"So are you, Zeus."

"Ah, but I'm a god. I'm harder to kill."

"But you *can* be killed?" I asked.

Before he could reply the answer came swiftly and terribly. Out of the silent air came a clattering rattle, sometimes known as a clattle.[32]

We had stepped out into a clearing – a circle where there were no trees and we could see open sky. That *should* have made us safer. Nothing could be hiding behind a tree ready to grab us. In fact it left us open to a new danger. Attack from the air.

The clattle came from a huge bird, but not like the Avenger – not like any bird you'd ever see on Earth. Its feathers were made of brass and its long beak was sharp as a javelin.

Just the brush of its wingtip shredded my shirt sleeve. I shuddered to think of what it might do to my

32 When I say known as a "clattle"... I mean it would be known as that
if there were such a word. But there wasn't until I invented it. It's my word.
If you want to buy it you'll have to go to a clattle market. If you steal it
you'll be a clattle thief... or a rustler. I could go on with jokes about you
growing your own on a clattle farm... but I won't.

skin the next time it dived.

But the creature wasn't interested in me. It was one of the monsters picked to kill Zeus.

In that first swoop that grazed me it struck hard at Zeus's face and carried something away to a nest of sticks it had built in a tree.

"It's taken my eye out," Zeus said and clutched at his face. The bird gave a harsh cry of joy and dived again. Zeus raised his sword but it hit the brass feathers and glanced off. The monster circled and swooped again before Zeus could swing the sword and it snatched at his sword arm with the brass beak.

Zeus's arm was carried away, along with the sword, and dropped into the nest. It was going to tear Zeus apart one piece at a time.

Zeus shook himself and changed into a shapeless blob of flesh. Then he changed back into a man… a man with two eyes and two arms.

"Ha!" I laughed. "It can't kill you then! You can just shape-change the pieces you've lost."

"It's not that simple," Zeus cried as the bird dived again and pulled off the arm that had just grown back. "I only have so much force to make my body. Every time he takes a piece I can change back into a man…

but it's a smaller man."

The bird ripped off the other arm. Zeus made himself into a shapeless mass again and then into a man. But I could see what he meant. He wasn't much bigger than me this time. If he kept losing arms at this rate he'd be no bigger than a mouse.

"What *is* it?" I cried.

"A Stymphalian Bird," he told me but his answer was cut short as the bird snatched off his head and cackled as it landed at the nest and rested.

I pulled the book from my pocket and looked in the back – the index section. I found the entry for 'Stymphalian Birds' and turned to it quickly. There was just enough light to read it.

"They go around in a flock," I said.

Zeus couldn't answer till he'd shape-changed again. He was smaller than me now. "No point in sending a flock," he panted. "They'd just get in each other's way. No, the Avenger knew what it was doing when it picked just one for this attack. Look out!"

This time the bird snatched both of the new arms Zeus had thrown up to shield his face. Now when he shape-changed he was no bigger than skinny little Alice.

The bird began to sing in a brassy warble, "The monsters, united, shall never be defeated!" Then it swooped again and as Zeus shielded his head the bird snapped off both of his legs and carried them away.

"Shape-change into a swan and fly away!" I told him.

"A swan?" he groaned. "I'd be lucky to make a pigeon with what I have left."

At last I found the page that told the story of the birds. I read it quickly as the monster sliced away Zeus's head again and left him so short he'd have had to stand on a chair to tie his sandals.

'Stymphalian Birds lived in the swamp at a lake in Arcadia. Two Arcadian warriors discovered they could be driven off with a loud rattle. They banged their shields with their swords, and shouted war cries to drive off the creatures,' I read.

The blacksmith used the travelling burner to repair pots and pans and to shoe horses. He made steel tyres for wagons, iron nails and farm tools. There were knives and forks, horseshoes and pans in the cart. I threw a horseshoe in each of the pans and ran into the clearing. Zeus stood between my legs and the bird shot at him like an arrow. I rattled the horseshoes as hard as I could and even in the dead air of the forest they made a hideous noise.

Clatter! Clatter!

The bird screeched in pain and swerved up to land on a branch. "Stop it! Please stop!" it cried.

I rattled the pans louder than ever and it tried to put its brass wings over its brass ears. "Spare me!" it croaked.

"No!"

Clatter! Clatter!

"I'm sorry, Zeus. Tell the human child to stop!"

I rested for a moment. Zeus stepped out and stretched up to my knee. "Take your brass-necked body back to Arcadia and leave this world in peace. If you are lucky I'll leave you in peace when I return to the Ancient World."

"And if I'm unlucky?"

"I will send my dear wife Hera to sing to you every night – if you hate clattering noises you'll hate that."

"I know," the bird moaned. "We've heard her as we flew over Olympus. I'm beaten, I know it. Goodbye."

"Wait!" little Zeus cried. "Before you go would you like to throw down all the body parts you've just ripped off me?"

"Ah, yes, sorry."

The arms and legs and heads (and sword) tumbled down into the clearing. Little Zeus struggled to put some of the largest arms into a neat pile... and I wasn't going to help move the blood-soaked mess.

At last they were gathered into a heap and the little god climbed on top. He changed himself into the shapeless blob and one by one soaked up the body bits. At last he had a full-sized blob and shifted it to the shape of a man again. He picked up the sword and shook himself to check that he was all there.

"Before you go, bird, perhaps you'd like to tell us what horror is waiting for us next?"

"I can't do that," the bird said softly (or as softly as a brass throat will allow). "Monsters of the world are united – and that means we don't snitch!"

"Ahhhh!" Zeus sighed. "I'd better call on Hera to give us a song!"

"No!" the bird squawked. "It's the Python. The Python is guarding the river. You'll never get across – and you have to cross it to reach Plough Rock. You've lost, Zeus. Lost." The bird clacked and clattled into the air. "The monsters, united, shall *never* be defeated."

Zeus tugged at the horse and led it down the road

that was signposted to Death. "Can't you just turn into a swan and fly to Alice?" I asked as we saw the trees thinning and the road rolling out ahead of us.

The god shook his head. "We need the blacksmith's wagon to break her chains – and we need the Gorgon's head to kill Cetus the sea monster. No, Sam, we are a long way from saving her yet… even if we do get past the Python."

That wasn't a cheerful thing to hear.

Zeus marched on. I'd saved him from the Stymphalian Bird and he hadn't even said thanks.

Maybe gods are too great to notice little human deeds, I thought.

We stepped past the last tree and saw the road winding down to the river. Zeus stopped a moment and rested a hand on my shoulder. "Thanks," he said.

FIFTEEN

THE TRICKIEST RIVER CROSSING YOU EVER SAW

Theus was back in Eden City. I'd love to tell you what he was up to but then you'd have to wait to see what happened when we met the Python at the river. In this world you can't have everything you want. In fact Theus will tell you that you can't have everything you want in ANY world! I promise to tell you about Theus soon…

The river started in the distant mountains, made from the melted snow. It raced over rocks but all that racing didn't warm it up. By the time it reached the plains of Eden City it was wider and slower. You could wade across it and it would come up to your neck – if you were my height – up to the waist if you were a tall man like Zeus. But your legs would be cool as a corpse when you reached the other side.

I was glad I had the wagon to ride in.

But when we crossed the river we would have to face the monster serpent that lay dozing in the midday sun. "The Python," Zeus said.

"Is he poisonous?" I asked.

"No," Zeus told me. "He just wraps himself around you and crushes you."

The horse seemed to understand and it shivered. Or maybe it was just the sight of the freezing water.

"So how will you beat him?"

"He's the easiest of all the monsters to kill," Zeus boasted. "I'll let him wind himself around me. As soon as he starts to squeeze me I'll slice my way through him with my sword. He'll walk straight into my trap."

"I don't think serpents walk anywhere – and it sounds as if you're walking into the Python's trap," I argued.

"You'll see I'm right," he laughed, took the reins and stepped into the water.

"Ooooof!" he gasped.

"Cold?"

"F-f-f-fresh," he said as his legs turned blue.

The horse didn't complain.[33]

When we reached the far shore the serpent stirred. "Good day, Zeus. Going somewhere?"

"Just passing," Zeus said and tugged at the reins to stop the horse by the water's edge.

The Python slid quickly across the path, his silvery body as slippery as seaweed and as strong as a steel spring. Zeus stepped forward and the spring coiled up around him. The Python made a loose loop of his mighty body and trapped Zeus inside. Zeus drew his bright sword from under his cloak as the monster made the loop smaller and smaller to crush him. Before the silvery body quite touched him the god chopped into it. The sword flew fast as a wasp's wing and carved a great wound in the serpent's side. In a moment he was halfway through the body and halfway out of the trap.

The serpent's eyes blinked slowly and his long tongue lashed lazily. Zeus took one last swing and cut through the last shred of skin. He was free of the crushing silver circle. He held the sword over his head in a salute of victory.

---

33 Which just goes to prove... something: Something about any old carthorse being tougher than the greatest god.

The Python's thin lips curled into a small smile.

"See?" Zeus called to me. "The easiest of all the monsters! Drive the wagon through the gap I've carved."

But I shook my head. I was looking over Zeus's shoulder. The path he had carved through the serpent's body had joined together again. It had healed without even a scar.

Zeus turned. He scowled. He raised the sword again and took a slice out of the monster flesh. He watched, worried as it joined back onto the body.

Then the serpent sprang again and wrapped himself in a circle around Zeus. He carved his way out and stood panting. Then Zeus backed away towards the wagon at the edge of the river. The serpent turned and looked straight at me.

But I didn't have a sword or the strength to cut my way free.

I turned the horse and whipped it into a trot back to the safety of the other side of the river. Zeus fled after me.

I stopped the horse and waited till he caught me. The serpent smirked on the far bank.

"He can make himself whole again – just like you,"

I said. "The Stymphalian Bird carried bits of you away before you could join together," I reminded him. "Maybe that's the way to beat the Python!"

Zeus looked angry. "The Python is a hundred times as big as me! It would take weeks to cut him up and carry the bits away. And we haven't got weeks!"

"Then we need something stronger than either of you to carry the bits away."

Zeus shook his head. "There's no one that strong."

I smiled and I told him my plan. Zeus looked at me. "You aren't stupid, are you?"

"No," I said.

"Let's try it," he said.

We worked together quickly. A mighty breath from Zeus heated the burner to a white-hot glow again. I took one of the metal wagon tyres and used hot lead to fasten knives and plough blades to the band. We fastened the finished band around Zeus's chest and the blades spiked out like a porcupine.

Then he stepped into the water. "Oooof!" he gasped.

"Cold?"

"F-f-f-fresh."

The important part of my plan was for the serpent to fight Zeus in the river – because it was the river that was stronger than Zeus or the Python. It was the river that would be our secret weapon.

Then I found there was a small fault in my plan.

The Python didn't want to come into the river to fight. Zeus was shivering. The serpent was smirking.

"C–c–come and fight!" Zeus called.

"You come here," the monster answered. "You're the one that wants to fight. I'm happy to lie here in the sun."

"You're scared," Zeus jeered.

"I'm not."

"You are a coward, you great fat ugly worm."

The Python's monstrous eyes opened wide. "Worm?"

"Yes. A worm can live after it's been cut in half. You are just an ugly worm."

The monster shuddered but it wasn't a shiver of cold. He was trembling with rage. "Stop calling me ugly, Zeus, or I may get angry. You wouldn't want to see me when I'm angry."

"Why not? Does it make you even *uglier*?"

I thought Zeus was doing a good job.

"Uglier?" the Python asked.

"Yes, you know. The Gorgons are so ugly their faces can turn you into stone. Well I guess you must be so ugly you'd turn anyone into solid brass! You're uglier than the Typhon's bum!"

The serpent moved quickly to take his revenge. He slithered into the water.

"Ooooof!" he gasped.

"Cold?"

"F-f-f-fresh," the monster said and made himself into a loop around Zeus.

Then he began to close around the god. Zeus didn't move. He let the loop tighten. The Python squeezed. He squeezed against the spiked band and the knives and plough blades sliced into him.

The tighter the beast squeezed the more he carved himself. Zeus didn't need to carry the chunks of flesh away. The river did that.

The fast flow washed away the lumps of slimy body before they could join back on.

Soon the Python's body was growing thin where so many pieces had been chopped from it. When it was thin as one of my weedy arms Zeus finally drew his sword and chopped downwards. The head was rushed out towards the sea – there were no brains to weigh it down. (It was a very ugly head – Zeus wasn't lying.) The tail, which was full of the victims the beast had swallowed, sank to the rocky river bed.

A monster in two parts isn't a lot of use to the T.Y.P.H.O.N. gang. The monsters, united, shall never be defeated. But the Python's head wasn't even united to his tail.

"The sun is past noon," Zeus said as he pulled off the spiked band and threw it onto the back of the cart.

He whipped the horse across the river. It stuck a little in the middle as we rolled over the Python's tail but we were soon back on the road to Plough Rock.

The path curved away to the coast and rose steeply. We found ourselves on a cliff road that wasn't much wider than the cart. To our left the cliffs fell away to the sea crashing on rocks a long way below. To our right there was a rock wall that a spider couldn't have climbed.

We couldn't go left or right. We couldn't turn round and go back. We could only go straight ahead.

Which was a pity.

Because a monster lay across the path.

It was a creature with the head and chest of a woman, body and legs of a lion and wings of an eagle. It was the lion legs and the slashing claws that looked the most dangerous. Zeus might be able to fight it but it would shred me and the horse before we could get a hair's breadth nearer to saving Alice.

"Will the lion legs tear us?" I asked Zeus.

"No," he said. "This is the Sphinx. It's the woman's arms that are her strongest part."

It was true the arms looked like Ma's.

"What does she do with the arms?" I asked.

"She strangles people. Wraps those mighty hands around the throats of travellers and chokes the life out of them."

I felt my throat go tight at the thought of it. "Nice," I croaked. "So there's no way past her?"

"Well, there is," Zeus said. "All you have to do is make a deal with her. Agree to answer her question."

"Question?"

"A sort of riddle."

I shrugged. "Sounds easy enough."

"No one has ever answered it before," Zeus said. "She is here to kill me – part of the T.Y.P.H.O.N. gang. She mustn't know who I am. She would strangle me, tear me apart and throw the pieces into the sea." He huddled into his hood – hoodled, you might say – and leaned on his stick like a weary old man. I had to face the Sphinx alone.

"We have nothing to lose," I said. "We can't just stay here looking at her!"

I stepped in front of the horse and the woman smiled at me. It was a nice smile. "Hello, little boy! My, you're a fine little boy. I bet your mother's proud of you."

"Well, yes!" I said and smiled back. This was going to be safe and easy!

"What can I do for you, little man?"

"Just let me pass," I said. "I'm off to save a girl called Alice."

"Oh, how sweet!" she cried and clapped her hands. The sound of the clap was a boom like doom. My doom.

"So if you'll just move aside, I'll be able to get to her before the sea monster."

"Love to, my dear child," she sighed.

I stepped forward.

"Just answer my simple question and you can pass."

"Oh, go on then," I laughed. "Ask away!"

"My! My! What a brave little boy!" she gasped.

"Brave? For answering a question?" I said and frowned.

"Ye-es. Didn't your friend in the cloak tell you?" she said and nodded at Zeus. "Answer my question,

169

and get it right, and you can pass."

"And if I get it wrong?"

"Why, I strangle you of course!" she beamed.

"Of course," I said and my legs went weak. I felt so giddy I thought I was going to topple over into the raging sea below me.

"Come and sit on my lion's paw," she purred. "It's lovely and soft. You'll be ever so comfortable."

The Sphinx took my hand and pulled me towards her. Her hand looked as soft as a dove's feather and felt as hard as the Storm Inn bread. It made me wish I was back there, sitting with my ma, not this monster woman-beast.

"What's your name?" she asked.

"S–S–Sam!"

"S–S–Sam? What an odd name! Now S–S–Sam, here is my simple little riddle. Are you ready?"

"Yes!"

"You're not worried?"

"Worried?"

"About being eaten?"

"Of course I'm worried about being eaten!" I squawked.

She smiled a lion-toothed smile. "You *mustn't* be,

little man! I strangle you before I eat you so you won't feel a thing! Now, doesn't that make you feel better?"

"Much better," I said. "Of course I'm sure I'll get the answer right."

"No one ever has," she said.

"I thought you said it was a simple little question."

"It's a simple question – but it's the answer that's hard," she growled and licked her lips. "Now, little Sam, here is the question. Which creature in the morning goes on four feet, at noon on two feet, and in the evening upon three?"[34]

34 It's all very well for you to sit there reading a book and saying, "I know the answer!" But YOU aren't facing a horrible death if you get it wrong. You aren't where I was: sitting on the knee of a woman with corpse-smelling breath. Or maybe you are! Awful isn't it?

SIXTEEN

OVER EDEN CITY – 1785 AT THE SAME TIME I WAS FACING THE SPHINX

Have you ever seen a snowball rolling down a hill? It starts small and slow and ends up fast and dangerous. That's what was happening with our story. While I was fighting monsters with Zeus, Theus was facing his own danger back in Eden City. I tried to piece together the story as it happened. If you want to follow it you'll have to have your wits about you… or be flattened by that snowball…

The Avenger circled high in the cloudless sky.

It had seen us send Cerberus for walkies,[35] shred the

---

35 All right, it had flown back to Ancient Greece. If you are being fussy you would not say "walkies", you'd say "flappies". It can be hard being a writer and trying to please people like you.

Python, then drive off the Stymphalian Bird. We just had to get past the Sphinx to reach Euryale, the Gorgon. The Avenger's plan was failing. Theus hadn't been tricked out of hiding.

But all good fighters have a second plan in case the first one fails. And the Avenger was a good fighter. It left me and Zeus facing the Sphinx. It didn't matter if we won or lost or if Alice was eaten. All that mattered was capturing Theus.

The Avenger headed back to Eden City.

It landed in the centre of the city beside a curious building. It was made of wood, like the others, but it was low and had curious pillars in front of a heavy front door. It had once been a town hall in the days when Eden City had been Eden Town. Now it was deserted... well almost.

The Avenger knew this place would become the Temple of the Hero one day soon. It knew it would be the place that Theus would come in search of the hero he needed to find. He had seen the future of Eden City on visits before.

The eagle pushed open the creaking door. A voice moaned, "I'm starving!"

The Avenger closed the door quickly behind it.

There was just one large room in the building. At the far end were dusty curtains, hung across a low platform. They might have been green at one time. High, dirt-crusted windows let in a little light.

On one wall was a list of mayors of Eden City. On another wall was a mouldering map of the streets.

A head pushed out between the curtains. It was the head of a bull. "I said I'm hungry!"

"Yes, Minotaur," the eagle said softly, "and you'll soon be fed."

"Children. I like children. They're nice and tender – not chewy like old people. On Crete they gave me seven boys and seven girls to eat."

"Yes," the eagle agreed. "But only once every nine years. I have ONE boy in mind for you to eat. He should be back in Eden City by nightfall if he defeats the other three monsters."

"The monsters, united, shall NEVER be defeated!" the bull-headed man argued and lashed his tail.

"Sadly three of the monsters, united, HAVE been defeated," the Avenger told him. "And I'm not too sure about the other three. *You* are the greatest monster of all."

"I am? Am I really?"

"Oh, yes. Everyone knows that."

"Greater than the Typhon or the Python?"

"They're both dead. That leaves you as the top monster."

"I always knew it," the Minotaur bellowed.

"All you have to do is eat this boy for me. You won't be hungry for much longer," the Avenger promised and headed for the door.

"Where are you going?" the Minotaur asked. "It's gloomy in here. I'm lonely. And it's scary!"

The Avenger stopped and looked back. "The Minotaur belongs in the labyrinth of Crete. Now the streets of Eden City are almost as twisting and tricky as a labyrinth," it said and pointed a wing-feather at the map. "All I need to do is place a few new fences across some of the streets and it will make a marvellous maze."

"That's clever," the Minotaur said and nodded his big bull head.

"I will hire a few ship-builders to build wooden walls. You will hear some hammering. Don't let it frighten you. I'll be back before nightfall," the Avenger promised. [36]

---

36 I have tried to put together this story from what the survivors told me. But one thing I never discovered was where the Avenger got the money to pay the workers who built those wooden walls. Sorry. It's one of the things that must remain a mystery.

The Minotaur shook his shaggy head. "I can't believe they'll beat the Sphinx," he muttered.

"Can you repeat the question please?" I said, stalling for time.

"Which creature in the morning goes on four feet, at noon on two feet, and in the evening upon three?" the Sphinx said. Her horrid hands twitched as they made ready to reach for my throat.

I looked back at Zeus for help. He rested on a stick like the old traveller of his disguise.

Then I remembered. I remembered the legend my ma told me about a king called Oedipus. He had to answer this riddle or die. The sight of Zeus leaning on the stick was the answer.

Do you know it? Here's a clue… imagine your life was one day long.

No?

Think about it. When you're a baby it's morning, when you're an adult it's mid-day and when you are old it is evening.

So…

"The answer is a human," I said.

The Sphinx shook. "What?"

"A human! In the morning of its life it's a baby and crawls on hands and knees – four legs."

"No!" she moaned. "No! No!"

"At noon we are adults and we walk on two legs."

"Please, no!" Her voice was rising to a scream.

I nodded back towards Zeus. "When a human is old it walks with a stick – a third leg."

"Aieeee!" she screeched and held her powerful hands to her tear-damp face.

"The answer is 'A human' – am I right?"

"No one has ever guessed! I am finished. I have no future. I have to die!" she cried and threw herself sideways off the cliff towards the sharp rocky shore below.

That would have killed me. It would have killed you!

But the Sphinx had wings on her lion body. The wind was caught under those wings and lifted her up. Soon she was gliding alongside us on the cliff path.

"I can't even kill myself!" she sobbed.

"Don't try," Zeus said, throwing back his hood. "Just fly back to Ancient Greece and behave yourself."

"The monsters, united…"

"Are now down to three," the god told her. "It was

a mistake to think you could beat the great Zeus. Now push off."

The Sphinx beat her stubby dragon wings and sailed off towards the sun. The path ahead was clear. I jumped back on the cart and we trotted up the path to the cliff top.

"Zeus," I said.

"Yes, my boy?"

"You told the Sphinx it was a mistake to think she could defeat the great Zeus."

"So?"

"So, it wasn't you that beat her… it was me!"

He sighed. "If she'd strangled you and started to eat you her hands would have been full. I was ready to slice her with my sword."

"That's all right then," I said. He didn't seem to notice the bitterness in my voice. "And I suppose you know how to defeat the Gorgon, do you?"

He shook his mighty head. "You and your clever book can tell me," he smiled.

"I'm sure we can," I muttered.

We were heading towards Plough Rock about a mile away but there were caves in the hillside that we had to pass. A movement caught my eye. I knew I shouldn't look at Euryale – I'd turn to stone - but I couldn't help myself.

I was lucky. She was still wearing the sack over her head.

She stepped out into the road, reached for the sack. Zeus turned the wagon quickly so even the horse had its back to her.

"Hello, boys," she said in a mournful voice. "You look nice."

"Thanks," I said and fumbled through the pages of the book.

"I've always wanted to meet nice fellers like you," she sighed.

"What stopped you?" I asked as I found the page on Gorgons.

"Well first all the handsome boys are put off by the bag over my head."

"I don't know why," I said. "It should add a bit of mystery. I've seen ladies in towns wear hats with veils!"

"Then the snakes sometimes pop out from under the sack for a peep. That REALLY puts the guys off," she said.

"Don't know why. Snakes are really cute."

"Not when you have them growing from your head," she sniffed.

"I've seen Ma when she hasn't washed her hair for a week and she looks a bit like that."[37]

"What's the answer?" Zeus hissed as Euryale twittered on about the men she'd loved and lost and turned to stone.

I read the page quickly. "You take your sword and you slice off her head."

"How can I do that without looking at her? I might chop off an arm or a leg by mistake."

"I'm coming to that… one hero took a polished shield and used it as a mirror. So long as you don't look directly at her face you'll be fine."

Zeus blew out his cheeks, annoyed. "Why didn't you tell me before we set off? I don't *have* a polished shield, foolish boy."

"Don't call me a foolish boy. I'm not here to look after you," I replied angrily. "*You're* the great god. *You're* supposed to be the hero. Why didn't *you* ask

---

37 If Ma ever gets to read this book I have to say I did not mean it! Honest!!! I was just trying to cheer up the Gorgon and keep her talking while I found the right page. Ma has always had fine hair flowing all down her back… none on her head but plenty on her back. Heh! Heh! Sorry, Ma, just another of my little jokes!

before we left?"

"There wasn't time," he said.

I turned very carefully and looked in the back of the wagon without looking back at Euryale.

"I met a really nice feller when I was on holiday in Spain. I think it was true love. I never took the bag off once. Then we went swimming together in the sea. It was lovely. Warm and blue. Really romantic."

"What happened?" I asked as I pulled one of the blacksmith's pans from the back.

"A wave washed the bag away. He took one look and sank like a stone... well, of course, that's because he *was* a stone. And stones make rotten swimmers. I swam back to shore and turned everyone there to stone too. No one goes to that beach to sunbathe any longer."

"Why not?"

"Too stony," she said.

I passed the pan to Zeus and he rubbed it hard with his tunic. It was soon shining in the afternoon sun and I could see the Gorgon's hideous face reflected. I didn't turn to stone.[38]

---

38 I'd tell you how hideous it was but you might turn to stone and you'd never find out how my story ends. Take my word for it she was gruesome. If you want to picture her ugliness then look in a mirror... heh! Heh!

"It works," I said.

"Then I will circle round behind her and cut off her head. Your job is to stop her turning round and looking at me."

"How do I do *that*?" I asked.

Zeus shook his head. "Look, I am the hero, I am doing the dangerous bit. Surely your simple wits can think of something to keep her mind off what is happening behind her?"

"Simple wits? You ungrateful..." I began to splutter, but Zeus had jumped down and was creeping towards the hill so he could circle round.

My simple wits were racing. How on earth do you keep a Gorgon amused?

What would *you* have done?

SEVENTEEN

A HILLSIDE NEAR PLOUGH ROCK

You may notice I've given you advice from time to time. One piece of advice was Ma's which said, "Face your enemy and nine times out of ten they'll run." Can I just change that a little? Can we make it, "Face your enemy and nine times out of ten they'll run — unless they are a Gorgon, in which case it is a bad idea to face your enemy otherwise you'll not be running anywhere — ever again." Glad we've cleared that up. Now let's get back to my problem… how could I keep a Gorgon amused?

I think my mind was turned to stone — not by Euryale the Gorgon's stare and not even by her sad chatter. It was the fear. The thought that those deadly eyes were on my neck. It sent a shiver through me like a wet rat up my trouser leg.[39]

My mind must have been numb because the answer to my problem was so obvious.

Ma and I spent nights in every city we visited keeping people amused. We sang and told jokes, and I recited my silly poems.

What was I waiting for?

"It must be very boring being a Gorgon… I mean apart from being lonely and unloved. You must get bored."

"I do, oh I *do*!" she sighed. "I mean, I tried reading a scroll. The first part was really exciting!"

"What about the second part?"

"I'll never know… the scroll had turned to stone so I never got that far."

"Sad."

"And I have to close my eyes when I eat or the food on the plate turns to pebbles. And I do like my food."

"What's your favourite?"

"Rock cakes."

"And you never see entertainers?" I asked.

"I watched a tightrope walker once. Wonderful.

---

39 If you've never had a wet rat up your trouser leg then you're lucky. Or maybe you should try it some time. For a laugh.

Then he turned and looked at me…"

"Turned to stone?"

"Mmm! Turned to stone – the weight snapped the rope and he fell straight down. He made a really deep hole in the ground. It took them weeks to dig him out."

"I'm an entertainer," I told her.

"Really? What do you do?"

"I recite poems."

"I like a nice poetry scroll… at least I like the first part. Tell me one of your poems!"

"It's a poem about a greedy little boy who eats till he's sick," I said.

"Go on, give me a laugh."

I gave her my favourite verse… and hoped Zeus wouldn't be too long.

I've had some plum pudding for dinner
All covered with sauce everywhere.
I had two big helpings that Mother gave me
And three more when she wasn't there.
Oh, I do wish that I hadn't ate it
I do feel so funny inside
You know, Mother said I was eating too much
Oh, I do wish that I hadn't tried.

I'm sure that I'm not fit for school - not today
But Mother says, 'Hurry up, Dick.'
So if she declares that I must go to school
I'd better, p'raps, try to be… quick?

I waited for a laugh. I got a sigh.

"One of my sisters, Medusa, was like that," she said. "She's not sick now, of course."

"Why not?"

"She's dead. Some hero called Perseus sneaked up behind her and chopped her head off using a mirror."

Of course I knew that. It was the story of Perseus that I had read in the book.

What Euryale said next turned my blood to ice. "Yes, he used the mirror trick… just like Zeus is doing now!"

I almost, *almost* turned to see but stopped myself in time. "Zeus?"

"Yes – we've come to kill him. The monsters, united, and all that."

"And will you?" I breathed.

"No," she said gently. "If he kills me then I'll go to the Elysian Fields. I'll meet Medusa… I may even meet that nice young man I met on the beach in Spain. The

Elysian Fields sound better than the draughty old damp cave I have to live in. I'll pick myself a better head and people will be happy to chat to me. Oh, I'll have such a nice t…"

Swish!

Thunk!

Moments later Zeus appeared at my side. He carried something in a sack.

"Two to go," he said, placing the sack carefully in the back of the cart.

The sun was dropping in the sky now. I knew we'd reach Alice before sunset. But I felt strangely sad at having to kill the Gorgon Euryale.

"Monsters have feelings too," I told Zeus.

He wasn't listening. "I'm getting pretty good at this hero stuff," he said as we trotted forward towards Plough Rock. "I've killed the Typhon…"

"With the help of Pan and Hermes," I reminded him.

He wasn't listening. "I've killed the Python and the Gorgon…"

"With my help," I said.

"… and I've driven off Cerberus, the Stymphalian Bird and the Sphinx."

"With my help," I repeated, but I was wasting my breath.

"I don't *need* Prometheus and his hero act!" Zeus laughed as we rolled up the Rock and saw Alice lying there, asleep.

I needed to try a new way of getting through to the god. "Imagine what sort of hero could rescue a hero," I said.

"What?"

"Imagine the legends they would tell if *you* were to rescue *Prometheus* from the Avenger!"

The god turned his golden eyes on me. "You think so?"

"Oh, yes. If you did that then I'd write the story myself. I'd turn it into a book..." I held up Ma's book of legends. "A book like this!"

Zeus looked pleased at that. "Then the sooner we free the girl and get back to Eden City the sooner I can rescue cousin Theus! Imagine his face when I do that! I'd never let him forget it."

"I bet," I muttered.

He blew on the charcoal burner till it glowed hot again and placed a link of the chain into the white heat. After a while he was able to strike it with a hammer and break it. Then we had to unwind the chain from around Alice and carry her onto the cart.

She opened her sleepy eyes and smiled. "Where am I?" she asked.

"You're going home to Eden City," I said.

"To Maggle's inn?" she asked. She didn't look as happy as she ought. If I had to choose between being a slave to Maggle the toothless landlord and supper to Cetus the toothful monster I might have only just picked Maggle. But I had to cheer her up.

"Perhaps Ma and I can take you with us when we move on… Ma always said she wanted a daughter."

Alice smiled sleepily. Then her eyes closed again and she lay back in the cart and dozed.

The horse grazed happily and Zeus stood on top of the rock staring out on the sunset sea.

The wind was soft and warm and the waves were just scarlet ripples.

Peace. But of course it couldn't last.

There was a small burst of white about a mile off shore. Something had broken the surface and was heading towards us like a long-necked whale.

"Cetus," Zeus said.

He stood with the sack by his side as the monster

drew closer. Cetus's eyes were too close together and his jaws too far apart. Never trust a monster with eyes too close together.

He reared out of the water and lunged for Plough Rock. He hung in the air, tail thrashing to keep himself high out of the water and roared, "Where's me supper?"

"Rescued," Zeus said.

"Aw, that's not fair. The Avenger promised me a nice bedtime snack if I came from Greece with him."

"The Avenger lied," I said.

"No, I can't believe that. It told us, 'The monsters have nothing to lose but their chains. We have a world to gain. Monsters of the world, unite' it said."

"It's your victim who's lost her chains," I said. "You monsters have been tricked by the Avenger."

Cetus shook his slimy head. "The Python tried to warn us that feathered fiend was no good. I feel really rotten now. In fact I feel a bit of a fool."

"You're not the only one. The Python and the Gorgon have already died for the Avenger's fight. The others have gone back to Greece."

"So what do I do now? I haven't got any wings – I haven't a clue what the Avenger did with my portable set."

"You can die, like your scaly friend the Python," Zeus said quietly and his free hand reached across to pull up the sack and reveal the Gorgon's face.

"I'd rather stay here," Cetus said. "There's something fresh and exciting about these waters – better than that clammy warm water round Greece. I could quite enjoy living here! Plenty of fish to eat."

"And humans on ships," I said.

"Nah! I think I've gone off human flesh – give me a nice fillet of haddock any day. We sea monsters sing a hymn for fish not flesh to preserve our noble queen."

"Noble queen? A *hymn*? About fish? What are you talking about?"

"Ye-es!" Cetus laughed. "Have you never heard us sing 'Cod Save the Queen'?"

"No," I said.

"Tell you what, Zeus, you let me stay here and roam the oceans and I'll tell you a secret."

"Very well," Zeus said carefully.

"The Minotaur is back in Eden City. He's going to kidnap a child and that'll get Theus out of hiding."

"When?" Zeus asked sharply.

"Tonight," Cetus said.

"We have to get back to warn him," I said.

Zeus gave a sharp nod and reached across again to uncover the Gorgon head and kill the sea monster.

I grabbed at his arm. Of course my puny body couldn't stop him but I think my scream of "No!" made him pause.

"It's only a monster," Zeus snapped angrily.

"You promised. You can't break a promise! You can't lie. Show some mercy. You're a great king."

"Don't be foolish. In Ancient Greece we break promises all the time. We cheat, we lie and we trick. It's what we do. So long as we win we don't care."

"But you're not in Greece now."

He turned on me and for a moment I thought he was going to show me the head in his anger. "I *know* I'm not in Greece. I'm in a country where cheats and rogues like you and your mother go around selling fake medicine…"

"Ah, but…"

"A country where weak children are made slaves of the strong…"

"I know, but…"

"And a country where you rebel against your 'great king' and you call it a War for Freedom. Am I right?"

"Yes, but…"

"So don't talk to me of kings and promises, lies and mercy."

The sack was hanging dangerously close to my face. The god was swollen with rage and he could have crushed me with one fist. Ma's voice rang in my head, saying, "Never show that you're afraid. Never back off from a fight, son. Face your enemy and nine times out of ten they'll run."

I took a deep breath and looked him straight in the golden eye. "Zeus, you *cannot* kill Cetus the sea monster."

He glared back at me and leaned forward. His breath smelled of the nectar drink and his face filled the sky. "Why," he asked, "not?"

I smiled gently. "Because he's gone."

Zeus seemed to shrink. He swung round and looked at the empty sea. Cetus had slipped away to find a new home and I hope he found some happiness too.[40]

---

40 He is still seen, of course. He roamed the oceans for many years and sailors reported seeing sea monsters. No one believed them but I am sure that was Cetus. The last I heard he had retired to a nice quiet life in a Scottish loch where the salmon are sweet and the weeds make beds as soft as silk. His eyes are probably still too close together, but somehow I hope he's happy and I'm sure he's never eaten anyone at all.

Zeus tore off part of Plough Rock in a rage and stuffed it into the sack along with the Gorgon's head. He tied a knot in the top and hurled it down into the sea. He gave me a godly glare and said, "If the Avenger plans to strike tonight then we'll have to hurry."

I made one of those stupid jokes to break his bad mood. "I'm sure the Avenger won't start without us!"

I didn't know quite how monstrously *true* those words were.

EIGHTEEN

RETURN TO EDEN CITY

You can sense that things are coming to an end now, can't you? That Theus and Zeus, the Avenger and the Minotaur were all going to meet in one final battle. Even as we clattered back down the darkening path I felt that too. What I didn't know was the part that I still had to play in this monstrous story. If I had known I might just have told Zeus that I'd stay on Plough Rock...

The moon rose and turned the road into a ribbon of silver. We rattled back along the cliff top – easy now with the Gorgon gone.

Zeus could have changed into a swan and flown ahead but he wanted the glory of riding into Eden City with the rescued maiden.

The cliff path was dangerous in the dark but at least there was no strangling Sphinx.

We struggled through the bat-black darkness of the forest with no Stymphalian Bird to bother us. The plash through the river was Python-less and we saw no Cerberus on the plains.

We could smell Eden City as its foul fug of fog drifted across to us. Alice shook herself awake and shivered. She warmed herself at the burner on the back of the cart while we told her the tale of the rescue. "I'll be the best slave you could ever wish for," she told me.

"Ma would never allow you to be a slave," I told her. "You would be our equal. One of us."

Alice shook her head. It was too hard for her to believe. I knew Ma would look after her. I didn't know that Ma was too worried to spare a thought for Alice at that moment. She was worried about her son, Sam.

She was afraid for *me*!

Why?

The people of Eden City had gathered into the largest open space there was – the square outside the city prison.

There was a platform at one end – a platform they usually used to hang their criminals.

But that night it was lit by flaming torches and Malachi Maggle, the landlord of the Storm Inn, was standing there waving a piece of paper.

"Citizens of Eden City, we face a terrible danger!"

"We know that, you fat fool," Mrs Grimble said. "That sea monster is going to wreck our ships if we don't feed it a child. We've already done that."

"We have!" the crowd agreed.

Ma had seen the crowds gathering in the street and had sensed there was more trouble on the way. Theus borrowed a cloak and wrapped it around his head in case the Avenger was out there looking for him. He stood alongside Ma at the back of the crowd.

"We face a NEW danger!" Maggle cried.

Ooooh!

"I have just had this letter thrown through the window of the Storm Inn," he said. "Let me read it to you… Hush-sh!"

People of Eden City
You have seen the power of Cetus.
Now see the power of a far more fearsome terror.

Now see the power of the bull-headed monster, the Minotaur.
The Minotaur chews children like mice chew cheese and he
is hungry now.
Send him a boy and send him soon or the Minotaur will
come looking.
Your old Town Hall is the place where the Minotaur dwells.
But do not follow the sacrifice in to try to save him
You may get in but you won't get out
At least not alive.
Signed,
The Minotaur

The crowd was worried. Parents clutched precious children to them and muttered in fear. Then they started chattering nervously as a figure pushed its way onto the stage and stood alongside Malachi Maggle.

The figure was odd and vague, like looking at a jellyfish through murky water. Some said it was an old man in a feathered cloak.

"It's an eagle!" Mrs Grimble told them.

"I have the answer to your problem," the feathered figure said.

"It's *not* an eagle, Mrs Grimble – birds don't talk!"

She wiped her grubby nose on her grubbier sleeve.

"Parrots do," she argued.

"You do not want to sacrifice one of the precious children of Eden City, do you?"

No-o-o!

"Then let me find you a boy from outside of the city – I know where I can get my claws on one right now!"

Ohhhh!

Maggle stepped forward. "Is it the wish of the folk of Eden City that our friend here finds us a stranger?"

Yes-s-s!

"Then go, stranger, with our blessing!"

Cheers!

Ma clutched at her mouth as if she were going to be sick. "Sam," she whispered. She swayed and Theus held her. He passed her into the care of Mrs Grimble for a moment, then pushed his way to the platform.

The crowd were about to leave – parents were plotting to hide their cherub children till the danger was gone.

"Stop!" Theus cried. "There is another answer."

Uhhhh?

"Someone could go into the Labyrinth and slay the Minotaur!"

"And risk getting killed?" Maggle squawked.

"I would do it," Theus said. "Give me a weapon and I will go."

A dozen old swords left over from the war were passed to Theus. He chose the brightest and the sharpest. "Show me the way to the old town hall," he said.

"Three cheers for… whatsisname…" Mrs Grimble croaked.

"It's Theus," he said.

"Three cheers for Theus, the only man in Eden City brave enough to face the monster."

"I would have done it," the blacksmith shouted. "But I have a bad back!"

"All right," Mrs Grimble cried. "Three cheers for Theus, the only man in Eden City – with a good back - brave enough to face the monster."

The crowd cheered and everyone wanted to slap Theus on the back and wish him luck.

"Wait!" came a voice from the back of the crowd. It was Ma. "Wait! It's not enough to go in and kill it. You have to get back out alive."

The crowd agreed that was probably impossible. But Ma had read the book of Greek legends. "Find me a ball of string," she said.

Time was ticking by but Theus waited while someone went to the quayside and took some strong twine from one of the ships. Ma tied it to the post of the platform and walked the way the Eden City people pointed. She marched past Theus towards the city.

"Just a moment," Theus cried. "This is *my* quest!"

"Ah," Ma said grimly, "but I think you'll find it's *my* son!"

Theus couldn't argue with that.

They set off into the lantern-lit maze of alleys, trailing the twine behind them.

If Zeus, Alice and I had reached Eden City under that umbrella of fog I'd have been safe from the people there. I was looking ahead to the first houses and the flicker of lanterns in the gloomy rooms.

I wasn't looking behind. I had no reason to look *above*. Nor had Zeus.

It was from the sky that the attack came. There was a *swoosh* of sound and cold breath of air on my neck. Then sharp talons dug into my shoulders and before I could open my mouth to cry out I was being lifted into the night.

I twisted round to see Zeus's astonished face and

Alice's fear then they disappeared as I was swept into the thick darkness over the city. There was no chance of Zeus following, even if he'd been foolish enough to leave Alice alone on the deserted road.

I was alone and being dragged between the smoke-churning chimneys of the twisted city. I knew I was being carried by some monstrous bird and I guessed it was the Avenger. What I couldn't guess was, what did it want with me?

It turned sharply and dropped steeply towards one of the lowest buildings in the city – a hall with columns at the front porch like a Greek temple. It dropped me to the ground in front of the porch. My legs were weak and it took me a while to rise to my feet. Lanterns hung from the front of the porch and showed me the ugly eagle that looked like a bent old man in a feathered cloak. "Don't try to run," the creature said. "The streets around here are a labyrinth. It's easy to get in but it would take you days to get out."

"Why have you brought me here?"

"Cheese," it replied.

"Cheese?"

"If you want to catch a rat you use cheese in the trap. You are the cheese."

"And Prometheus is the rat you hope to catch?" I nodded.

"Your mother will have guessed that her little Sam has been taken prisoner. Prometheus will search for you. As I said it will be easy enough to get into the Temple here, but he'll never get out alive."

I looked around the square. The misty air was still and dead. The Avenger pushed at me with a powerful wing and forced me inside the building. There was a powerful smell of cattle in there. A curious monster sat on the platform at the end of the candle-lit room. His man legs dangled over the edge while his huge bull head looked as if it would topple him over. His nostrils snorted out foul air and his eyes burned red and hungry.

His bull mouth slobbered. He began to move.

"No!" the Avenger said. "Not yet!"

"You promised."

"As soon as Prometheus is in my grasp you can have the boy – it's his *life* Prometheus wants to save. If he finds the boy *dead* then Prometheus will save himself. So do not touch the boy or I'll destroy you!"

"Destroy me?" the bull head howled. "I'm a monster – a brother. We're united."

I'll swear the curved beak curled back in scorn. "Believe that if you like. *I* am your master and you'll do as *I* say. Now give me your belt."

"My belt?"

"I need something to fasten the boy to a pillar," the eagle said coldly.

"I can't!"

"You *will*," the Avenger hissed. "I am your master and you will do as I say!"

"But my kilt will drop down!" the bull-man-monster moaned.

"Oh, tie a knot in it. Now hurry! He will be here soon."

The Minotaur hurried to obey and soon I was strapped to one of the pillars.

The Avenger calmly walked across to the doors, its hooked claws clacking on the dusty wooden floor. It stood behind one of them. There was little hope that I could see. Theus would walk through the door and the Avenger would take him.

Then the Minotaur could eat me.

Simple really.

NINETEEN

EDEN CITY – 1785

Let's just leave me there to be eaten, shall we? Why would you care? I had risked my life to save Alice the slave-girl. Was it worth it? Before I died I'd like to have known that my monster battles were worth something. That I had died for a reason. No one wants to die for nothing.

Zeus stopped by a stream and gathered some water in his cupped hand. He looked hard at the water and it began to take on a golden glow of nectar.

He held it in front of the nose of the weary horse and it lapped it hungrily. Suddenly the horse found new strength to rear up and paw at the air. It snorted and set off at a gallop before Zeus had climbed back on the wagon.

He scrambled aboard and he and Alice clung on as they raced through the rutted streets.

It seemed as if some streets in the centre were blocked off so it took them a while, even with a charging horse, to find their way to the quayside. The horse skidded to a stop outside the Storm Inn just as Malachi Maggle was opening it for evening business.

"Get to work, girl," he snarled at Alice. "If you're not going to get eaten by sea monsters you may as well earn your keep."

Alice found the courage to shake her head. He took a step towards her and raised his hand. Zeus caught the blow easily in the palm of his own hand. "Mr Maggot, this is important and we don't have much time."

"Ouch! Ouch! Ouch! You're hurting me. Leggo! Leggo!"

Zeus ignored him.

"Have you seen a bird…"

"There was pigeon on the roof this morning but I think that sea monster scared it off."

Zeus squeezed, Maggle screamed.

"A large bird like an eagle – but it could be mistaken for an old man in a feathered cloak," Zeus prompted.

"Yes! Ouch! It *ouch!* Went *ouch!* To get a boy *ouch!* For the Old *ouch!* Hall – some Minot-*ouch* creature wanted a sacrif-*ouch!* The bird feller went to help us *ouch!* Leggo!"

"Where will we find the town hall?"

"Follow the twine from the prison square, ouch! Ouuuuuch!"

"Where's the prison square?"

Alice tugged at Zeus's arm. "I know where that is," she said.

Zeus nodded.

"Will you let go of me now?" Maggle moaned.

Zeus smiled. "Of course." He raised his arm in the air and lifted the landlord off the ground. Then he swung him twice around his head before he let go. The fat man flew over the quayside and into the greasy water of the cold river. By the time he struggled ashore the river was greasier.

"Show me the way to the square," Zeus said.

"Wait," Alice said. "We need something from the Storm Inn." She hurried through the door and came out moments later with a bundle under her arm. They ran off into the night.

The Minotaur looked at me, his red eyes burning with hunger. "You could have brought me a fatter boy," he moaned. "This one is only a couple of mouthfuls."

"Hush!" the Avenger ordered. It stood behind the door and bent its head to listen. Then it stiffened. It was a few moments before I heard what the bird had heard. Two sets of footsteps walking over the porch outside. The heavy door creaked open slowly.

I saw the sword first, then Theus. He smiled at me. Ma burst past him and ran to me. "You're still alive, Sam!" she sobbed.

"Not for long," the Minotaur said.

Ma stood between me and the monster. "If you want to hurt Sam you'll have to kill me first," she said.

"Fine," the bull replied. "I don't mind that. I was just saying the boy's a bit too weedy to make a good meal."

I could feel Ma trembling in front of me but couldn't see anything – she's a big woman. "Theus!" I called out. "The Avenger. He's behind the door. Save yourself!"

Ma stepped aside so I could see what was going on. The door swung shut and the Avenger stood in front of it. "The bait worked," it hissed. "You are mine at last, Prometheus."

Theus lowered the sword. "At least let the bait go. You have me. Set Sam and Mrs Wonder free."

The Avenger looked across at me. "I may as well – unfasten the boy," he told Ma.

"Here! That's my dinner!" the Minotaur bellowed.

Theus raised the sword. "No. I'd kill you before you could touch the boy," he said.

"That's not fair," he roared.

Theus walked across to the bull-man. "Heroes save victims… monsters die… it's the way of the world," he explained.

Ma nodded and said, "That's the way it happens in the books."

"It's not fair," the Minotaur muttered and bowed his head, ready to die.

"Sam wasn't the bait to get me into the Avenger's trap. *You* were, Minotaur. It just used you."

"But we're brothers. Me and the Avenger. Brothers. Monsters… united."

Theus shook his head sadly and walked over to the platform at the end of the room. He scooped up a pair of Olympus wings and handed them to the Minotaur.

"Take your wings and fly back to Greece. There's a hero called Perseus waiting for you there."

"Can I have my belt back, please?" the monster asked meekly. "I can't fight this Perseus if me kilt falls down."

Theus unfastened me and passed the belt to the bull-man.

The Minotaur took the wings silently and slipped them on. He walked to the door and the Avenger stepped aside. "You lied to me," the Minotaur said sadly.

"It's what monsters do," the bird sneered. "Get out. Go to meet your doom the way the stories say."

The Minotaur shook his shaggy head and slipped out into the night. The Avenger looked at Theus. "That was a mistake, Prometheus. You could have used those wings to escape yourself."

The eagle took one slow step towards Theus. Then another. It began to spread its wings as Theus lowered his sword and waited.

That was the moment when the door burst open. Zeus rushed in and Alice stumbled in behind him. She threw the bundle under her arm at Theus – it was his wings. "Fly, Prometheus, fly!"

The Avenger moved to stop him but Zeus shape-changed into a long snake and coiled himself quickly around the Avenger. He pinned its wings to its side. Zeus's snake head said, "Fly, Prometheus!"

"You can't fly forever!" the Avenger screamed and writhed in the clutches of Zeus's coils.

"He's right," Theus said as he slowly strapped on the wings. "It never gives up. I may as well die now as tomorrow."

"No, Prometheus," Zeus said. "We know that this place will become The Temple of the Hero. All you have to do is find that hero and you are forgiven. Come back here in one year and there *will* be a statue to a hero here. One year, Prometheus. One year." The snake head twisted to look at the cruel face of the eagle. "Do you agree, Avenger?"

The eagle head nodded once. Zeus shifted back to his godly shape and set the Avenger free.

"Can we come back a year from now, Ma?" I asked.

"We can, Sam. You can't have a story without an ending."

She wrapped a warm arm around my shoulders and led me to the door. That's when we heard the sound of voices in the little square outside. The sound was growing louder all the time. It was the sound of a crowd gathering and growing.

"It seems as if the people of Eden City have seen the Minotaur fly away," Ma said.

Theus held up a hand. "Wait… I'll check that it's safe, make sure the Minotaur has really gone, " he said and he stepped out.

Why did he have to do that? I suppose it's what heroes do – they take the lead.

I could have stepped out first, or Ma, or Zeus or Alice or the Avenger. The first one out would be the one the people would cheer.

But it was Theus.

And it was to be the beginning of the end for him.

The crowd of Eden City people were crushing into the square outside the old town hall. As soon as they saw Theus they burst into a long cheer.

"Here he is!" the blacksmith cried, pushing his heavy body to the front of the crowd. He stepped onto the porch, gripped Theus by the wrist and raised the arm with the sword into the air. "Our champion! This is the man who drove the Minotaur into the skies. The monster took one look at whatsisname here …"

"Theus," Theus said.

"The monster took one look at *Theus* here and flew off. The children of Eden City are safe and it's all down to Theus. Three cheers for Theus!"

The crowd cheered loudly again. When they had settled the blacksmith cried, "Let's all go to the Storm Inn to celebrate!"

"How do we get there?" Mrs. Grimble asked.

"Follow the twine out of the maze the Minotaur made," the man told her.[41] The happy crowd spilled out of the square and one group lifted Theus up onto their shoulders. "Careful! Watch his wings!" a man called.

"Wings? Where did they come from?" a woman asked.

"He didn't have them on when he went in," the man said.

"I suppose it's because he's a special sort of man," the woman replied. "We'll never forget him, that's for sure."

The party at the Storm Inn went on most of the

41 Yes, YOU know the Minotaur didn't build this labyrinth. YOU know it was the Avenger. Well, clever pants, I know that too. But the people of Eden City believed it was the Minotaur's work, didn't they? Now stop trying to pick faults with my book and get on with the story.

night. When the morning came Theus stepped outside and stretched his wings. He hugged me and then he hugged Alice and then Ma. (She liked that.)

"One year and we meet again at the old town hall," he said. "What will you do till then?"

"Carry on travelling, selling medicine and putting on shows. We have a new actor in the team," Ma said and smiled at Alice.

The shows had always been exciting. Now they'd be dull compared to hunting monsters, rescuing maidens and being rescued.

Still, there was next year to look forward to.

Stories have to have endings, Ma said. Theus would find his human hero and the Avenger would be defeated. I knew it was going to be a happy ending.

Which just goes to show how little I knew…

EPILOGUE

EDEN CITY – 1786

A year later. Of course you'll know how the story ends. You don't have to read on. You've had all the clues so you can see what is going to happen. I was wrong and you are probably right. I don't know why I didn't see it coming.

We met at the Storm Inn. It hadn't changed – it could have been a little grubbier but that would be hard. We had changed. Alice had grown. With Ma's care she was more sure of herself and she made a great actress in the shows.

I suppose I had grown more confident too. If a strangling Sphinx and a powerful Python can't defeat you then you get to think nothing ever will.

We walked down the gloomy roads and alleys of

Eden City under a sky of dirty slate and past shuffling, squinting people. The old town hall had been cleaned up and a sign over the porch said, "The Temple of the Hero".

Inside there were rows of seats where I guess people would go to pray or worship the hero. On the platform there appeared to be a tall figure but it was covered by a white cloth to keep it free of the grimy Eden City air.

The Avenger was lurking behind the door. It swung it shut after us and pushed a bolt.

"So we won't be disturbed," it hissed.

Prometheus in his wings and his cousin Zeus stood by the figure under the cloth.

We smiled and greeted one another. Theus looked thoughtful and Zeus restless.

"Ready?" Ma asked.

She raised the cloth a little. Words were carved on the base of the statue.

"The Hero – he saved us."

I grinned at Alice and winked. I was so happy and so stupid. "Here you are, Theus! A human hero. This is the person who was so brave they raised a statue to him . . . or her. This is the hero who's going to save you!"

Ma raised her hand and swept the cloth away.

I stared at the figure and the smile slid off my face.

It was a statue of a man. A tall, strong man. He looked like a human, except for the wings.

The face was a handsome one, and one I knew. It was the face of Prometheus.

We were silent.

From the back of the temple there was a soft clatter as the Avenger clapped its wings in happiness.

"Not a human hero after all," it hissed. "A demi-god. There are no human heroes – that's why they had to invent gods! Fools!" The Avenger turned in triumph. "I think you have lost, Zeus."

The king of the gods looked in agony. "No! Give Prometheus more time."

"He's had all the time he's going to get," the eagle said and snapped its beak angrily. It clattered on talon-tipped feet down the aisle towards Prometheus.

Zeus stood in its way. "I won't allow it."

The bird snorted. "You cannot stop me. If you try I'll take your life first and then I'll take Prometheus."

"You can't threaten me. I am king of the gods. There's no one greater. I cannot die."

"Oh Zeus, you only live because these humans

believe in you," the Avenger said sweeping a wing at where I stood clutching the book of Greek legends. "When humans stop believing you'll die."

Zeus seemed to shrink at the thought.

And then, too late, I saw it all. "There is *one* greater than you, Zeus," I said softly and looked at the great golden bird.

"That's just the Avenger – it's only a servant of the gods – what I'm thinking of *is* your servant and the gods *do* use it. But it is not the Avenger."

I turned and looked into the eyes of the creature. Eyes as deep and dark as a well.

"Tell them your real name," I said.

The rounded shoulders shrugged. The twisted neck turned and looked at each of us in turn. "The boy is right. I call myself the Avenger but the name that everyone knows me by is… Death."

Theus smiled a little sadly and nodded. "Life is a road… a wild and wearying road… and I've reached the end. Death is like an old friend, waiting at the end, to wrap me in his arms."

"A friend?" I cried. "He takes away the ones we love."

Theus looked at us with a sad smile. "No. He

brings us all together. I am going first. But I'm not leaving you… I am just going to another place to wait for you. One by one you'll join me." He looked at his cousin. "Even you, Zeus. One day, when the humans stop believing, you will join me."

"I know," Zeus murmured and clasped Prometheus to him.

One by one we lined up to hold the hero for one last time. "And me," I said. "Wait for me."

Prometheus nodded. "You most of all, Sam. I'd never have fought the monsters without your help. That should be your statue there, Sam. You and Alice. Zeus sent me to find a human hero… and, truly, I found *two*!"

I opened my mouth to tell him he'd won the challenge but he pressed his finger against my lips. "No, Sam. There is a time for leaving. Nothing lasts forever. And I deserve my fate."

"You were the only god to care about us," I said. "You gave us humans fire!"

"And you turned it into smoke that chokes the air and weapons that kill the innocent," he sighed.

Zeus rested a hand on his shoulder. "I tried to stop you. The humans were too foolish to understand about fire. One day, when they are as old as the gods, they may be wise enough. But not yet, Prometheus. Not yet."

Theus shrugged.

He walked to the door and stepped outside. We followed. Theus looked around the gloomy city and up into the sky. It was one of those rare days in Eden City when the sun shone down and warmed the square in front of the Temple. He didn't turn and look at us. He simply said, "I'm going home. Goodbye."

The Avenger stepped behind him and wrapped its golden wings round the god. It crushed him till the life that was in him fled. Then it took the limp body in its massive talons, beat its wings and lifted into the air.

"Where are you taking him?" I cried.

"To the Elysian Fields," the Avenger said.

"I'll never forget him."

"No, but he will forget you. In the Elysian Fields heroes live forever but forget their life on earth. They forget the pain, the fear, the heartache and the misery, the hunger, the cold and the cruelty."

"We'll remember him. All of Eden City will!" I argued.

The Avenger shook his head. "Memories are short. You'll soon forget."

And then I knew what I had to do. I had to write down the story of Prometheus. If it took me twenty years I'd write that book and tell our story. The book of legends had taught us how to fight the threat of the monsters. Now I had to write a book that would teach the world what my adventure with Prometheus had taught me.

A book that says there's always hope. A book that shows a hero lives inside us all. Even a foolish boy like me or a feeble girl like Alice.

A book... like this.

I looked at Theus one last time. At rest. "Goodbye, my best friend," I said.

The bird-shaped monster rose towards the clouds over Eden City. "In the end I am the kindest friend you'll ever meet."

It gave a curious cackle, as if it were trying to laugh but didn't know quite how. "I am Death. The friend of humans, gods and heroes. Goodbye... for now," it croaked as it vanished into the sun. All I could hear was the beating of my heart and the faint farewell, "For now. For now!"

GLOSSARY

The Avenger/ The Fury: An eagle with god-given powers, it was commanded by Zeus to rip out Prometheus's liver every day.

Cerberus: Monstrous dog with three heads who guarded the entrance to the Greek Underworld.

Cetus: A terrible, flesh-eating sea monster.

Delphyne: Half girl, half dragon. Temporary guardian of Typhon's cave.

Euryale, the Gorgon: One of three Gorgons, an evil snake-haired monster who would turn anyone who looked at her to stone.

Hecatonchires: A giant Greek monster of incredible strength and ferocity. It had 100 hands and 50 heads.

Hera: The queen of the Olympian deities. She was wife and sister of Zeus. Hera was mainly worshipped as a goddess of marriage and birth.

Hermes: The son of Zeus and the messenger of the gods. It was his duty to guide the souls of the dead down to the Underworld.

Minotaur: Bull-headed, savage monster living in the maze of King Minos of Crete.

Pan: The half-goat, half-human son of Hermes. This Greek god liked to eat, drink, play music on his flute and indulge himself.

Prometheus: A Titan who stole fire from Zeus and the gods. In punishment, Zeus commanded that Prometheus be chained for eternity in the Caucasus. There, an eagle would eat his liver, and each day the liver would be renewed, making the punishment endless.

Python: A ferocious dragon, represented as a serpent.

Sphinx: Half woman, half lion and a riddle poser, she ate anybody who answered incorrectly.

Stymphalian Bird: Violent, bloodthirsty flying monster with brass feathers.

Typhon: One of the most terrible of all Greek monsters, a man with one hundred dragon heads and snakes attached to his body.

Zeus: The youngest son of Cronus and Rhea, he was the supreme ruler of Mount Olympus and of the Pantheon of gods who resided there. He upheld law, justice and morals, and was the spiritual leader of both gods and men.

ABOUT THE AUTHOR

Terry Deary writes both fiction and non-fiction. *The Fire Thief* was his 150th book published in the UK, this was followed by *Flight of the Fire Thief*. *The Fire Thief Fights Back* completes the trilogy.

Terry's books have been translated into 28 languages. His *Horrible Histories* series has sold 20 million copies worldwide. Terry has won numerous awards, including Blue Peter's Best Non-fiction Author of the Century.

Terry lives in County Durham and has one grown-up daughter.